Also by Lydia Millet

Omnivores

LYDIA MILLET

George Bush, Dark Prince of Love

A PRESIDENTIAL ROMANCE

Scribner Paperback Fiction
PUBLISHED BY SIMON & SCHUSTER
New York   London   Sydney   Singapore

SCRIBNER PAPERBACK FICTION
Simon & Schuster, Inc.
Rockefeller Center
1230 Avenue of the Americas
New York, NY 10020

This book is a work of fiction. Names, characters, places, and incidents either are products of the author's imagination or are used fictitiously. Any resemblance to actual events or locales or persons, living or dead, is entirely coincidental.

SCRIBNER PAPERBACK FICTION and design are trademarks of Macmillan Library Reference USA, Inc., used under license of Simon & Schuster, the publisher of this work.

Designed by Brooke Zimmer
Set in New Baskerville
Manufactured in the United States of America

10 9 8 7 6 5 4 3 2 1

Library of Congress Cataloging-in-Publication Data
Millet, Lydia, 1968–
George Bush, dark prince of love : a presidential romance / Lydia Millet.
p.   cm.
1. Bush, George, 1924– Fiction. I. Title.
PS3563.I42175G46   2000
813'.54—dc21   99-35606
CIP

ISBN 0-684-86274-3

The author wishes to thank Maria Massie, Sarah Baker, and Marah Stets for their confidence, and Randolph Heard for keeping her honest.

For Saralaine and Nicholas, who made laughing easy

George Bush,
Dark Prince of Love

Prologue

Some women like muscle. Brute strength, or the illusion of it. Their idea of an attractive man is a craggy meat-packer with a squirrel brain, who likes to crush vermin with his bare fist. I call these women Reaganites.

Now, the Reagan-loving women are not weak. That's a popular misconception of what I like to call the Liberal Bourgeoisie. Oh, they may like cooking and value their Tupperware; they may often be Episcopalians; they may gather together in white A-frame houses to fashion Liberty quilts on the first Sunday of each month. But they're the ones working at little needlepoints of the flag while the local maniacs burn crosses on the neighbor's lawn, and smiling quietly. They tend to be long on purpose, but short on delicacy.

Personally, I've always preferred the underdog. I was the plain girl with buck teeth and pigeon toes in the corner of the schoolyard, offering her recess snacks to the skinny boy with glasses and a stutter. There was something about him—call it gentility or call it a pathetic quality—that caught me and held me.

And that's what sets me apart from all my Reagan-loving sisters. Sets me apart, and sets me free.

For the language of true love is not carnivorous. It's not florid. It is not words like *plunder, pillage, kill the Communists.* It is a kinder, gentler language, of nostalgic longing; it speaks of a more subtle mastery. And yet it harkens back, at the same time, to our long history of savagery. Without which we'd be nothing but hippies. It is a language that tells us what to think, like lords with serfs in olden days, but asks for our indulgence, too. It hints that we can visit savagery as if we were tourists.

It is a language, I contend, like "Read my lips."

I see that you doubt me.

1989

1. The Great Inauguration

Our funds are low . . . we will make the hard choices,
looking at what we have and perhaps allocating it differently.

—PRESIDENT GEORGE BUSH,
Inaugural Address

G.B.'s inauguration cost $25 million, the most expen-
sive one in U.S. history. But you have to celebrate
democracy. Without rites and ceremonies we're
nothing but a bunch of apes in fancy outfits.

I had followed the '88 election campaign closely from
the very day I was let out of jail, where I'd been languishing
for eight long years, wasting away among reprobates while
the Flower of my Youth withered and died on the vine. And
that was really a shame, about my Youth. Because up till then
it had been one of my best Qualities. They don't include
"pretty" or "nice." What can I say, you play the hand you're
dealt.

Let me set your mind to rest: I was innocent of all
charges. Now, I'm not saying I'm the Holy Virgin. In fact, I
wouldn't even make the grade as one of those fallen women
that were frequently anointing Jesus' feet. The Bible's big
on prostitutes who give pedicures, and those ancient scribes

had a real way with words, which I fully appreciated during my brief tenure in Women's Max Sec since the New Testament was all we were allowed to read. Minus the Book of Revelation, which the warden claimed might incite us to violent acts. Apparently it had triggered a group-psychosis episode among some Seventh-Day Adventist inmates, who got fed up waiting for Armageddon while they were on laundry duty and tried to tumble-dry a small-bodied Muslim to death.

No: I have a mean streak, a devious personality, and when I'm in my cups I can enjoy a good fistfight if the cause seems just. I'll be the first to admit I have faults; they just don't include a tendency to commit criminally negligent homicide. Sure, convicts often protest their innocence while counting the months till their next shooting spree, but that's not me. If I was guilty, I'd say so. I'm going to tell the plain truth, because you deserve it. And I respect your moral sensibilities.

What happened was, I had a friend named Shelly. She was my best friend ever since second grade. That was when we learned there was safety in numbers; I blackmailed her stepdad and she bribed my mom, so they both left us alone. By the time we were eight we were running through the neighbors' sprinklers in identical bikinis. We didn't look the same: Shelly was scrawny but beautiful, even then, and I was already wearing Ladies' Plus Sizes. I tend toward obesity. When we hung out together we looked like a stick and a balloon. But Shelly never shunned me for that. She would beat on kids who called me Fatso and Lardcake.

Anyway, I was the bookworm and she was the slut. I cheated and stole and got us into state college, where, in our dorm room, she made out with a guy named Bonanza on the third day of classes. By prearrangement I was hiding in the slatted closet to see what it was like. I'd never kissed a guy. But Bonanza had a pelt of fur on his back that would have made a mink jealous, and Shelly had drunk some Wild

Irish Rose. So when she saw it she leaned over the side of the cot and threw up, if you'll pardon my French. Later we laughed in the shower room and did some crystal meth she'd bought from him. That was the kind of friends we were. Inseparable, pretty much.

When her second divorce came through we celebrated at Bowl-o-rama. We bowled gutter ball after gutter ball, because we were higher than kites. Afterward we decided to make a beer run, and I got in the driver's seat. Ran a red light at an intersection, and we were hit from the right.

The coroner's report showed Shelly was pregnant at the time. She hadn't known it. Her aunt Rachel, who had always hated my guts and once shaved Shelly's head to teach her chastity, testified that Shelly was a good Christian girl. Aunt Rachel was a pro-life activist and liked to throw fetus dolls smeared with ketchup at teenage girls on their way into Planned Parenthood clinics. I still remember staring at her as she sat there ramrod straight on the witness stand: she wore a ruffled, floral-print blouse and had her hair sprayed into rigidity. It sat on her head like a boxy gray helmet. She said, "My niece had never taken illegal drugs before that night. She was coerced by peer pressure. Michelle was a very innocent and pure person and a faithful churchgoer. She was a bright, shimmering angel."

Then Aunt Rachel burst into tears and covered her face with her hands.

Well, at the time I was so depressed about Shelly that I could barely speak, but I had to laugh aloud at that one. Shelly would have.

It was no belly laugh—more of a pained choking sound. But the jury did not appreciate it.

And of course I had the priors for shoplifting paint thinner, possession with intent, and assaulting an officer. Two of which Shelly had shared with me. That telltale fact was not mentioned at the trial, since Aunt Rachel had sicced the victims' rights advocates on my wuss of a Public

Defender. My own legal guardians were notably absent from the trial proceedings, but that didn't surprise me. They were doing the same thing they'd done all my life, which was watch TV.

I don't need to tell you prison didn't bring out the best in me. I failed repeatedly to have my sentence commuted for good behavior. The thing was, I knew Shelly's death was an accident and all, and that it would have been me in the passenger seat if her ex hadn't stolen her Hyundai the week before. And frankly, I wished it *had* been me. Shelly always had better prospects. So for the first two years I wallowed. I felt responsible, and I missed her.

Anyway, right after I got out in early fall it was election year, and I watched the Presidential campaigns and the televised returns avidly. I'd forgotten that I lived in a Country during my years inside; I had forgotten the colors and the ceremony. It was still a novelty to stroll in the fresh air, under the sun or moon, without Bessie G. putting me in a headlock for the sake of a broken Kool, or having to watch T-Bone practice her full-contact yoga on the new recruits. I was colonizing the Land of the Free, and I felt downright patriotic. Every night when I got home from the factory, I liked to nurse a gin and cranberry juice, put my feet up and watch the news. Then I'd take a walk through the mobile-home community and look at the sky.

Of course, everyone knew the outcome before Election Day; Dukakis didn't look like a President. That's one thing about Presidents: they can be spotted from far away. If I had seen Dukakis in a teeming mass of people before he gained the Democratic nomination, I might have said "podiatrist, with orthopedic specialty." Depending on his garb, I might have said "professor of political science" or "poultry supplier to the greater Boston area." But of all the P-words, I would never have said "President." I suspected that two wiry tufts of hair had recently been pruned from the Dukakis ears in preparation for camera close-ups. And I was not alone.

G.B. was a shoo-in.

For the Inauguration, I laid in my own supplies: some Fritos, marked down to thirty-nine cents because they pre-dated Stalin, and a bottle of Baby Duck. I decorated the trailer with some old Christmas-tree icicles. My social calendar was not full. In fact, it looked exactly like a *TV Guide*.

I've always had mixed feelings about TV. It's kind of like when your parents are alcoholics, and their poison of choice is bourbon. Now, if you decide to follow in their footsteps as an Alcoholic, you don't go reaching for the bourbon. Not right off the bat anyway. You take your own path in life, maybe Scotch or good vodka.

So because I grew up with parents who were fixtures in front of the pixels, I used to avoid it like the plague, which is why I grew up reading books. But in jail I had a lot of printed materials and not enough TV, plus which the small screen was the only access road to the Great Beyond. I started getting into it finally. And when I got out and had no one to talk to, I was hooked.

At that early date, I was not yet a smitten woman when it came to G.B. Up until the Inaugural I'd pretty much thought of G.B. as the wimp with the Willie Horton ads. Sure, there was the appeal of "Read my lips," with its mild-mannered yet primitive simplicity. But basically, I hadn't thought twice about G.B. I saw him as a Reagan hangover, and unlike my fellow citizens, I had never cared much for Ronnie. Maybe I was just in a bad mood from being in prison, or maybe, by dint of being inside, I was immune to the raging Gippermania that hit the country. You tell me.

Whatever the case may be, the Inaugural was a turning point. When G.B. exhorted us to "as a society . . . rise up united and express our intolerance," I was intrigued. It may have been the Baby Duck, but this struck a chord. I struggled to my feet, slopping a yellow lip out of my flimsy plastic cup, and toasted the sentiment. I saw myself in the vanguard of an intolerant army, cutting a wide swath across forested lands with our bulldozers as we headed for the Capitol to mass beneath the West Front terrace where he spoke. With the soapy taste of cheap champagne in my mouth, I wasn't a hundred percent sure what we were intolerant of, but this seemed less important than the call to arms.

The bottle emptied steadily, and I was finally forced to switch to gin. At that point I became an expressive participant in the dialogue. G.B. would ask, "Are we enthralled with material things, less appreciative of the nobility of work and sacrifice?" And I would say, "No, sir."

Or he would say, "My friends, we are not the sum of our possessions." And I would say, "Hear hear. If we were, I'd be a 1973 Plymouth with busted suspension and a dirty beige Goodwill couch."

Or he would say, "There are young women to be helped who are about to become mothers of children they can't care for and might not love. They need our care, our guidance, and our education, though we bless them for choosing life."

And I would say, "Bless you, sluts." And I would say, "Ever hear of a condom?"

I was emboldened by drink. And alone. But the way he looked, it was as though he'd heard me.

There were blots on the landscape, admittedly. Such as VP Dan Quayle, G.B.'s retarded son. In political terms. G.B. himself regretted the choice just days after he made it, writing in his diary, re VP D.Q., "I blew it." But let's face it, bagging on D.Q. is like kicking a three-legged dog with chronic flatulence. I'm above it, frankly. Charity begins at home, and G.B. took that motto to heart. He believed in helping the disabled. As he said that very night, we have to hold out our hands to the less fortunate. "The offered hand," he said, "is a reluctant fist, but once made, strong, and can be used with great effect."

I went, "I'm there, G.B. I'm there."

And then I danced, lost my footing, and fell against a lamp shaped like a cowboy hat, breaking the bulb.

I was in a delicious, blurry mood when I finally settled down to sleep on the lumpy futon I'd found in someone's garbage pile and deloused with a spray can. The lingering smell of fumigant reminded me of chlorine. I thought of the swimming pools of my childhood, with Shelly sitting on the edge and dipping a toe in, me eating a Creamsicle beside her, and other kids' mothers in lawn chairs behind us shining with coconut oil. (In the summertime, Shelly used to choose her boyfriends based on which rich kids in our classes had pools. We would narrow it down to the best three or four pools by word of mouth, then case the joints one by one before Shelly made her selection.) Suddenly the image came to me of G.B. presiding over a million acres of rolling green hills and white colonial homes, dotted with kidney shapes of cool blue. He stood on a pedestal not far away, arms crossed, nodding slightly, a rigid baron of decency. I was balanced on the end of a springboard, waiting to plunge into relief and luxury. I was bouncing in anticipation, on the balls of my feet.

I don't know exactly how it happened, but somehow in that picture the joke froze. I stopped laughing at G.B. It was like a door swinging on its hinges, but not quite closing. For the first time since T-Bone had bent my left thumb backward and broken it, I slept dreamlessly.

And I was so hungover the next day I could barely make it to the assembly line. Working where I worked then, you came into contact with some unsavory types, though to be honest they compared quite favorably to both T-Bone and Bessie G. By sheer dint of the fact that they washed regularly. Still, I was unpleasantly surprised when, in the morning, several of my coworkers took it upon themselves to crassly impugn G.B.'s capacity for leadership. One of them went so far as to pin a typed quote to the Employee Information bulletin board beside the snack machine. *I have my own opinions,* it read. *I just don't always agree with them.* It was attributed to our new Commander in Chief. A misquotation, I was confident. Either that or G.B. was engaging in a little good-humored self-mockery, too subtle to be understood by the plebs. For a President, he had a lively sense of humor. You can't take these things out of context.

G.B. and I had shared a silent communion after the Inaugural, and I was irritated. People these days don't give a President an even break. Everyone and his brother has to have an opinion on every damn thing. Everyone thinks they're the expert. They'll talk shit about a President behind his back, but you can bet that if he reached out to shake their hand at a shopping mall, they'd be as excited as a kid on Christmas Eve. They'd be relating the experience to friends and relatives until they were senile and nodding in their armchairs. "Did Grampa tell you about the time he met the President?" And once they'd shaken a Presidential hand, they'd hesitate before they talked the same old shit again.

It pissed me off. Of course, the guys I worked with were a far cry from the residents of Greenwich, CT, G.B.'s home turf. They wouldn't know blue blood from gutter trash. G.B. was full-fledged American aristocracy, but all they wanted was a raise and a health plan. No vision. It would have broken G.B.'s heart if he'd seen it.

I decided to take a stand for unity.

At first my method was persuasion. For instance, there was a guy who worked up at the loading dock and liked to whine on and on about wanting a leg prosthesis for his crippled kid. Now, I respected his needs, but it was his only topic of conversation, besides sports scores and the supremacy of the white race. So one day I cut him off, took him aside, and said, quoting G.B., "Tommy, good faith can be a spiral that endlessly moves on."

Tommy goes, "Huh?"

So I said, "Freedom is like a beautiful kite that can go higher and higher with the breeze."

Because I'd committed several key passages from the

Inaugural to memory. But forget it. The words were wasted on him. He spat on the ground and went back to his forklift.

When I saw that poetry wasn't working, I knew I might have to abandon persuasion and resort to force. That came to a head when I punched another coworker in the stomach defending G.B. It was a bad move, and I regretted it almost right away. But I have a temper, as I may have mentioned previously, and she was making remarks about his private masculinity that I thought were disrespectful of the Leader of the Free World.

Luckily I coopted another phrase from the Inaugural at the dispute arbitration, which convinced my supervisor I was a reasonable person. "Lee Ann," I said, "I'm really, really sorry. And on days like this we remember that we are all part of a continuum, inescapably connected by the ties that bind."

Lee Ann said, "Fuck ties, you crazy bitch," but my supervisor, who'd just taken sensitivity training, was moved and docked Lee Ann's pay instead of mine.

Thank you, G.B.

2. Heavenly Peace

On June 3–4, 1989, more than 1,000 unarmed protest-
ers were killed by government troops in a massacre that
crushed China's emerging prodemocracy movement.
— *Webster's New World Encyclopedia*

I don't think we ought to judge the whole People's Lib-
eration Army by that terrible incident.
—PRESIDENT GEORGE BUSH,
four days after Tiananmen Square

I came to think G.B. would be a great guy to have on
Neighborhood Watch. In the afternoons he'd dress like
a crossing guard, wearing an orange reflector vest, and
route heavy commercial traffic into other streets; at night
he'd chase down burglars wielding a streamlined little rifle
with a high-end infrared scope. And he'd be popular for
not sticking his nose into other homeowners' private business. Take wife-beating, for example. You wouldn't see G.B.
barging into the next-door neighbor's house to stop him
bludgeoning his wife.

No, G.B. had an honor code. It was all about respect for
your fellow world leaders: a gentleman's agreement. A simple and streamlined philosophy that I knew well from my
time in Max Sec. This is a dog-eat-dog world, and we regular
people are surrounded by butchers and thieves. You hold
your head high, move forward through the dark, and flatly
refuse to be distracted by the glinting blade at someone
else's throat.

That happened to me the second month I was in Max, while I was still in shock over the transfer. They had moved me from Min solely because I defended my person against an unprovoked aggressor in the kitchen. By the time they told me I was being transferred, I'd heard enough about Max to know it would have been wiser to lie there and let my face be scraped raw with a four-sided cheese grater. But it was too late.

Anyway, the glinting blade was Tiananmen Square in a nutshell, the way I saw it. Like me, G.B. had held a steady course. Much as I had walked right past Rump, who then was T-Bone's girlfriend, as she nicked an Agg Assault inmate quite near the jugular with her clumsy shank, he had walked past the massacre. Much as I had greeted Rump cordially in the morning—fearing the loss of a few much-needed meals if I showed open disapproval of her unseemly conduct—he had sent his National Security Adviser to Beijing after the incident, to be photographed "cheerfully toasting Chinese party officials." Rump, at 320 pounds and most of it muscle, was even heftier than me, and that girl liked to eat. China is over a billion strong, and has nukes.

Enough said, I think.

As Deng Xiaoping put it in a radio address, "Bad people mingled with the good, which made it difficult to take the drastic measures we should take." He was talking about how they opted not to roll over the students with tanks, which I thought was a solid call. And to the Liberal Bourgeois naysayers in the U.S. press, clamoring sanctimoniously for punitive action, G.B. said coolly and with Firm Resolve, "This is not the time for an emotional response."

I should tell you right up front that I've harbored a grudge against the Liberal Bourgeoisie ever since my trial, when the victims' rights harpies had screwed me. (It's a hard term to spell, so from now on I'll just say L.B.) I gleaned the expression from a fellow prisoner in Min, who'd been locked up for defrauding elderly Christians with fund-raising junk mail. She fancied herself some kind of revolutionary, though she lived off the dividends from inherited stock in the Coca-Cola Company. She was always going on rants against the L.B., which included her family, and her funny lingo stuck with me.

The way she saw it, there was the L.B., the P.B., and the G.P. The P.B. being the Petty Bourgeoisie, the G.P. being the General Public. She had it all worked out into pie charts she said were based on Karl Marx, split into wedges that represented segments of the country. The L.B. were largely Democrats, the P.B. were Reaganites, and the G.P. were either illegals, illiterates, or didn't have time to vote. They were the silent majority.

Anyway, as far as the L.B. goes, as she liked to say, it's easy to pretend to love your fellow humans when you don't have to shower with them. Or give them your money.

The early summer of that year was winding along slowly. Humidity and torpor wrapped me like a shroud. I was getting used to my freedom, and starting to forget it. I worked double shifts and on weekends to build on the measly three hundred bucks in my checking account. Sure, I was being paid a minimum wage, which was more than I had made in the Pokey; sure, I had almost four hours a day for leisure. "Do with them what you will!" said my country, generously.

But there were errands to run and bills to pay, and the days ran together into one straight line. Straining under the yoke of routine again, all I had was the factory and its citizenry.

My job would have been better suited to a mechanical arm. I folded corrugated cardboard into box lids and put the lids on crates of lawn-tractor parts as they passed me on the belt for sixteen hours a day. Now and then I would imagine something surprising leaping out of a box the second I secured the lid: one day a dwarf with psoriasis, the next a chicken with a frog for a head. And then I'd jerk my hands back quickly so that it couldn't grab me.

But that got old fast, so I tried to comfort myself with

the knowledge that most jobs get tedious, over time. This one was a crash course in monotony, but for all I knew that was a blessing in disguise. Better to know now that you're an automaton, I reasoned, than to only realize it thirty years later, as is often the case with those who pursue the loftier white-collar professions.

As for the citizenry, they were untouchables. You wouldn't want to touch them even if they let you. Which they didn't. Lee Ann was the best of the lot, and she wasn't speaking to me since our dispute arbitration. Understandably, since the supervisor had been picking on her pretty constantly. I made a number of sincerely apologetic overtures, explaining that I was a hotheaded patriot and had a fledgling but proud allegiance to G.B. I offered her the chance to hit me back, but she just stood there with her arms crossed, frowning.

I went so far as to bring her a chocolate cake with multicolored sprinkles that I'd baked myself, from a mix. It featured almost an inch of marshmallow frosting, which I knew she preferred to all others. She ignored me, so I took the cake home again and ate the whole thing in one sitting.

It was too bad, though. Before her slander of G.B., I'd figured maybe we could get to be friends. She had confided in me once or twice from her workstation, which was next to mine, on personal matters and had written me out a couple of her home recipes. Her husband had recently died in an accident—I'd even been invited to the funeral, along with everyone else from our shift—so she was alone many nights. Like me, Lee Ann wasn't exactly your average prom queen; she had a melanoma on her cheek the size of a quarter. Also, she appeared to be suffering from male-pattern baldness. She may have resented my full head of hair.

I found I was beginning to look forward to G.B.'s sound bites and public appearances with the childish curiosity and appetite I had formerly reserved for Seabreezes, monster-truck rallies, and all-you-can-eat breakfast buffets. It was a secret fulfillment, almost as satisfying as the rushes I'd known in olden days, when Shelly and I used to pop her coveted amphetamines in the dirt lot behind Frat Row and then break in through the back door while the rich boys were fast asleep and count the boners. Shelly would lead the way through the silent bedrooms pointing her flashlight at the sheets and going, "No, no, no, no—yes!" That kind of adolescent caper just tickled her pink. But since the accident, I've never done another drug except one time. I'm reformed, in a manner of speaking. I was only along for the ride anyway. I would have jumped off a bridge if she had told me to. I'm not exaggerating. I'd done worse.

I settled into a nightly practice that I called G.B. TV. It went like this: I would get home, take a shower, and sit in a ratty lawn chair on the four-foot plot of prickly grass in front of my trailer, sipping my first cocktail and watching the sunset. Sometimes, while I sipped, I would exchange a pleasantry or two with a neighbor. There was an aging ex-hooker named Mimi, who owned a trio of grimy brown poodles and was an adherent to the Bahá'í faith, and a welder with four missing fingers, living off worker's comp. We didn't have a lot of common ground, so we bantered about the weather, taxes, and the other neighbors.

Then I would enter the kitchen, boil up my three pouches of Lean Cuisine pasta, and take them to the sofa with my second cocktail, to munch placidly on my various Cuisines until G.B. made his entry into a news segment.

When that occurred, I would cast aside my Fettuccini Alfredo temporarily and talk to him straight. We had a back-and-forth almost every night. Some nights he didn't speak on camera, having been videotaped in passing as he busied himself with golf or matters of state; in those instances I would just kid him quickly or pump my arm in his direction with a hearty cheer or two. After he disappeared from the screen, I would channel-surf and further discuss the issues of the day with commentators on CNN, the *NewsHour,* or *Nightline,* with a focus on such subjects as pertained to President 41 and his Administration.

These exchanges could become heated arguments when I'd had one too many, but were usually matter-of-fact. One informed, analytical citizen to another. "Well, Ted, I can't agree with you there," I would say, shaking my head regretfully. Or, "My Democrat colleague hasn't done his homework on this one, Peter." I observed the process carefully and mimicked the intonations of the experts. Before long, I felt I blended in perfectly. At that point, my rapport with G.B. was more or less a casual hobby.

And then Lee Ann was fired. It wasn't wholly due to the fallout from our dispute; she was a sluggish, disinterested worker and took two cigarette breaks every hour. True, the supervisor hadn't appreciated her brief verbal outburst at the arbitration, being an avid Born-Again and not a fan of profanity, but I did not feel Lee Ann's word choice was my responsibility.

Two nights after her termination, when I finished my second shift, she was waiting in the parking lot with her brother-in-law and his friend, a sheriff's deputy. I approached them in an open fashion, thinking this was an opportunity to commiserate over her joblessness and maybe offer to spring for a farewell drink or two, but they had a different agenda. They chased me into a corner, where the brother-in-law fractured my shinbone with a length of lead pipe. Then Lee Ann sat on my chest and forced me to eat a pack of Virginia Slims. Menthol. It was nearly full.

It was while I had eight or nine in my mouth that I came to the realization that, however much we all may like to frolic in the sunflowers with two fingers in a *V,* singing "Give peace a chance," there are some individuals who just won't. Peace has to be a two-way street. You can't have a unilateral declaration. Sometimes the gentler lambs among us have to find that out the hard way.

3. Ich Bin Nicht Ein Berliner

When Gorbachev allowed the Berlin Wall to collapse, Bush denied himself considerable political capital by refusing to go to Berlin and capitalize on the victory.

—MICHAEL R. BESCHLOSS

Wouldn't be prudent.

—GEORGE BUSH

G.B. is a man of taste and discretion, which is the one thing about him that's un-American. They say hindsight is 20/20, and you can bet that if I'd been his policy adviser in November 1989, I wouldn't have let him get away with saying, "I'm not going to dance on the Wall." I would have told him to forget his diplomatic ties to foreign Communists. After all, come 1992 he was gonna have an election to win. I would have told him to stand right up on that rusted Iron Curtain for the CNN cameras and take all the credit.

But I was distracted at the time. I had a new boyfriend— or "companion," I guess you could call him. He wasn't a Greek god or anything, but he was company. The last flesh-pressing I'd done in person before the kite of freedom flew over the skies of Eastern Europe was in 1982. And on that particular occasion it was what you might call involuntary, on my part at least. If I recall correctly, the guard was pretty gung ho. You don't find suitors as polite and self-effacing as G.B. in our nation's penal facilities.

My companion was young in spirit, but by the calendar he had a few decades on me. I met him on Halloween in a drugstore, where he was purchasing cherry-flavor antacids. We stood together on the checkout line. He noticed I was buying a large number of small Eveready batteries, on special sale, and made some off-color remark. Then when I didn't bat an eyelash at his crudity, he suggested we had interests in common and should take in an adult movie.

At first I was a little hesitant—even, though I feel guilty saying it, disgusted. Love may be blind, but let's face it: lust has eyes in the back of its head. He talked through a voice box due to having had a laryngectomy and tended to remove his dentures and reglue them at the dinner table. Still, I hadn't engaged in social behavior for years, which is unnatural for mammals. And after all I was only doing what G.B. had recommended patriotically in his inspired Inaugural, i.e., "harnessing the unused talent of the elderly." To do him justice—Russell, not G.B.—he did have talents, once the teeth were out.

And he had tender moments, too. Sometimes when he was musing on his service in the Korean Conflict, I got choked up. The first time we shared a tin of Planters peanuts and a bottle of Black Label, he sang "We Shall Overcome" through the voice box and I sat listening to him in the dark and started to cry silently. Then we danced to an old bagpipe recording of "Amazing Grace" that Russell had on vinyl until we got tired, collapsed onto the ground, and fell asleep.

In terms of social intercourse, Russell was even more hard up than me. His wife had left him back in the late seventies and joined some kind of nunnery for lesbians in Costa Rica. He subsisted off Social Security and only owned three shirts; it was a miracle he didn't inhabit an appliance box between two garbage cans. Luckily for him, a rich daughter who hated his guts had died intestate in her fifties and he was the only family they could find. So he lived in an actual house, which had belonged to her. It was a nice house, too. Five bedrooms, a backyard with a hammock, and a wraparound porch. Periodically, he would sell off a portion of her valuable antique-furniture collection to support his recreational cocaine habit.

I say "habit" because when I met him it was not an addiction. Twice, three times a week tops. For a man his age, with not too many interests beyond sex, drugs, alcohol, and abusive practical jokes, Russell in those early days had remarkable self-control. He had the appetites of a much younger guy; he was thin as a rail, grizzled, and full of metal joints and plates that were souvenirs of his time in the Marines. And I have to say that, except for the War on Drugs, some aspects of which he was apt to rudely denigrate as "fucking unconstitutional," he had appropriately high regard for G.B. That was important to me, even if it was based solely on G.B.'s promise not to "tinker" with Social Security.

Because after the incident with Lee Ann, I'd begun to feel there were some urgent problems in the country requiring G.B.'s personal attention. Call it a lack of morale, call it the disintegration of honor. It wasn't so much the physical pain of the attack that bothered me, in retrospect; it was the fact that I'd been forced to check into the hospital for my fractured shinbone and minor concussion, which depleted my meager bank account and put me in debt to the tune of almost a thousand bucks.

G.B. was preoccupied with foreign affairs, so I saw it as my duty to clue him in to the facts of life here at home. I launched a targeted letter-writing campaign, composing a series of briefs and policy memos to the White House. These were well researched and contained testimonials from my life experience as an average citizen and member of the G.P., including an account of the lead-pipe episode. They carried headings such as "Re: Working Class Alienation in the

U.S.A." or "Re: Rehabilitation and the Repeat Offender." When Russell asked me out on our first date, I hadn't yet received a response and was becoming a little morose.

Russell—or "Russki," as his Marine buddies used to call him because of his weakness for Stoli vodka—had some sterling qualities. He didn't make me go out in public with him, partly because he never went out at all except to buy food, pharmaceuticals, or liquor, partly because he was happiest either performing unclean acts or lying in the bathtub in a drunken stupor. At night, when he was high, he'd head for the roof and shoot off his old service revolver toward the constellations. "See that?" he'd go. "I got Orion, right below the belt." Senior citizens have a reputation for dignity that is largely unwarranted.

Once, when a neighbor complained, the cops knocked on the door and Russell opened it wearing a plaid dressing gown and a hearing aid he never used, and carrying a giant picture Bible with large print, from which he read the cops a parable or two. Just so they'd think he was a cute old codger. I must admit, it worked. They chuckled, patted his shoulder, drank some hot chocolate before they left, and let him off with a fond warning. As soon as the patrol car turned the corner, Russell had dropped the Bible facedown in the foyer and was doing lines right off the kitchen table. In some ways, he reminded me of G.B.

He was tolerant of my small eccentricities, he liked full-figured women, and he was undemanding in terms of physical intimacy. Also, sometimes he would curl up on the dining room floor in the middle of the afternoon and go to sleep in the fetal position. It was an endearing custom.

I started spending more and more time at Russki's. It was much roomier than the trailer, and he was always nodding off and leaving me alone to pursue my hobbies. And in his own way he really appreciated me. I had a study of my own in the basement that he didn't go into. He wasn't the nosy type. The basement study functioned as a clearinghouse and vault for information on, and memorabilia of, G.B. It was there that I composed my memos, letters, and briefs to the White House, and there that I conducted my research on current political events, with books I carted home from the public library. It was also there that I set up a modest exhibit devoted to G.B., which I thought of as a homemade folk museum.

The crowning touch to the decor was a big cross I made out of rotting planks I found in a dumpster. I tied them together with twine and nailed the whole assemblage on the wall. Then, in the middle at the top, where the traditional initials go, I etched a new series: G.H.W.B. I made a lifelike effigy and stuffed it with pillows and Styrofoam peanuts; onto the front of the head I glued a life-size, blown-up photo of G.B.'s face, smiling uncertainly.

And from then on, whenever G.B. got crucified in some L.B. rag, I made it literal. I hammered in a rusty nail for every print-media blow he suffered at the hands of the L.B. By the time Iraq invaded Kuwait, the effigy looked like a porcupine.

But I'm racing ahead again, in my girlish anticipation.

Russki and I did have our arguments, which is healthy— up to a point. You should always express yourself. The arguments were usually caused by his jokes; I didn't share the Russki's sense of humor. I would go over to his place, tired and sore from a long day at the factory, step wearily through the front door, and find my head covered in a bucket of pig manure. Russell would laugh to beat the band, weeping from mirth, slapping his good knee and doubling over in his armchair. Laughing isn't easy for a guy with a voice box, and neither is it pretty.

His boyish pranks were the only thing, other than the procurement of controlled substances, that he ever expended energy on. He would go out of his way to buy fresh fertilizer or trip wires for his elaborate tomfoolery. Mostly by mail order, true, but it still required initiative. We had a knockdown, drag-out fight after my middle finger was nearly severed in a rat trap. He'd hidden the trap in dead Sarah's vintage 1930s breadbin; I reached in to get some Wonder bread for our French toast, and whoops-a-daisy! I was in shock for ten minutes. It hurt like hell.

No matter how pissed off I got, it didn't make a difference. Russell would do a few quick lines while locked into the bathroom and then, gibbering like a monkey, chase me around the house with a flyswatter until I stood my ground and walloped him. At which point he'd turn gray in the face and collapse, and I would be the one with the bad conscience, given that he was over seventy. So I'd pick him up, dust him off, and tuck him into bed with a cup of hot lemon tea and a drop of whiskey. But the next day it'd be the same thing all over again. Every week I was either enduring humiliation or nearly losing a digit.

I talked to G.B. about the situation, soliciting his advice. His own domestic order was not dissimilar to mine; he was also partnered with an individual who was, for all intents and purposes, a member of an older generation. Though by the book she was one year younger than G.B., B.B. was "everybody's grandmother"—including his. G.B. was no spring chicken, but he had a boyish way about him—an aura of eternal youthfulness that marks only the scions of the leisured classes and the clinically insane. In Russell, who was neither, it was brought about purely through chemical agents.

B.B. was G.B.'s grandparent, virtually, and Russell was old enough to be mine. While I was fairly certain that B.B. did not indulge in practical jokes, I assumed she was the source of other conjugal irritations for G.B. Although I had no proof, I imagined her propped up on their ample bed pillows next to him, adjusting her reading glasses and nattering on about her "crusade" to "stamp out illiteracy" while G.B. was trying in vain to concentrate on a fact sheet about chemical warfare.

So I asked G.B. what he would do in my position. At that time I was developing a number of communication techniques, which involved subtle and silent acts of ESP. I would say to myself, "Okay, after I count to forty-one the next thing G.B. says applies to me." It worked admirably. I watched him closely for a coded answer during a newscast that was ostensibly devoted to fiscal policy, and I found one: give Russell a taste of his own medicine. I planned and executed it, if I may say so, flawlessly, by substituting antifungal foot powder for his stash inside the hidden Ziploc baggie.

Unfortunately, he didn't clue in until he was on his third line. One trip to the VA hospital later, I was the joker with the last laugh. Except I wasn't really laughing. When we got to the emergency room, they said he looked bad, but I knew it would take a helluva lot more than tough-actin' Tinactin in the sinuses to knock Russell out. And I was right. It took him a few days to recover—peaceful, tranquil days. He lay in his canopy bed staring glassy-eyed at the ceiling while I made myself at home in Sarah's hardly used Jacuzzi.

And having struck a blow for equality, I began to feel sorry for G.B. It was becoming clear to me that his marriage, like his choice for the Vice Presidency, was a misguided gesture of charity. He and B.B. were wax statues in a museum, standing side by side and smiling plastically—she in her knotted neckerchief decorated with the red, white, and blue flags of the world, he in a worker's hard hat worn during the election campaign, when he toured a factory.

I had no doubt that a genuine, comfortable affection persisted between them: B.B. was good-humored, and she could take a joke made at her expense. But I did not detect an all-consuming, forceful passion in their rapport. In private moments, I believed, B.B. would dandle the Free World Leader on her knee.

Anyway, when Russell came out of it, he was a sport. He'd seen some action in Korea and was no stranger to injury. He barely remembered the low-grade seizure, and the period of invalidism hadn't really fazed him. He chortled good-humoredly at my craftiness and then we were right back to the same old prankster routine. You can't teach an old dog new tricks. Three days after he was on his feet again I found my toothbrush Krazy Glued to my tongue.

The point I'm making is that I achieved a balance in my life right then. There was heaven, represented by my confidant G.B.—another, better place that looms above us in the sky and offers solace—and there was earth. Earth was represented by Russell. On earth, sometimes you have to deal with pig manure; on earth, sometimes you lose a section of your tongue. Also on earth, not every willing, eager man talks with the vocal chords God gave him. Or eats with the teeth.

4. Operation Just Cause

Bush sat down to lunch with Noriega in 1976.
  —KEVIN BUCKLEY, *Panama: The Whole Story*

I've said it's not true, he's said it's not true, and people
who weren't at the meeting, for reasons of their own,
[are] questioning the veracity of me and him, and I don't
understand it . . . but I know how it works.
  —PRESIDENTIAL CANDIDATE GEORGE BUSH,
                                        May 1988

I admired G.B.'s outright-denial tactic when it came to
that Contra business. I took a cue from it and used the
tactic in my own life. On one occasion, for example, I
had an opportunity to skillfully deploy it when I drove Russell to the notary public at the mall to have him sign over
the title to his house to me. The notary, who, might I add,
was none too sharp, said, "Is this gentleman currently
under the influence of alcohol or medication?"

It was a fair question. Having consumed almost a full
bottle of Jim Beam, Russki could hardly walk. His head was
lolling sideways on his shoulder like the hunchback of
Notre Dame.

I said, "Certainly not. My uncle is a veteran. He has a
nerve disorder."

She said, "Are you positive?" busily filing her rainbow-
colored nails.

Russell had turned around and wandered over to a pot-ted ficus, which he was gazing at fixedly as he swayed back and forth. I took his arm gently and guided him to the counter again.

I said, "Uncle Russell, please tell the nice official lady. Do you drink liquor or abuse illegal substances?"

Russell's chin jerked off his collarbone like he was under interrogation by the DEA. "Fuck no," he said, and that was that. The other witness was a kid I gave ten bucks to, whom I had found outside trying to scratch his name into some mall customer's gold Mercedes.

Clearly, that was a case in which a White Lie fostered a Greater Good. If Russell hadn't signed over the deed to me, he could not possibly have expected to shuffle off this mortal coil with satisfaction, in the knowledge that he had made a positive contribution to Society. For all the joy and home-cooked meals that I had brought to him, one measly house was a small price to pay. And although Russell had never specifically said that he desired to leave his house to me, or even that he wanted to make a contribution to Society, it seemed to me that both of these were foregone conclusions. I've read that dying men often regret, if only for a fleeting instant, their wasted lives, and I didn't want that to happen to Russell, in a moment of Supreme Clarity as the light shone forth and angels sang.

The next day he didn't seem to remember, though, so I decided not to dwell on the issue. I planned to reassure him when the time came—if we were still together then, and I hoped we would be—that his affairs were all in order, and that he'd be remembered both nobly and gratefully.

But anyway, the Panama Invasion taught me a lesson. You can only lie down and take abuse for so long; sooner or later you have to strike back. Here we had a homicidal Dictator killing and torturing dissidents, nullifying elections as quick as you can say "democracy," drunk as a skunk every day of the week, and getting millions every month in military aid from Uncle Sam. And then, as if that weren't enough, he cops an attitude. At a party one time Noriega said, of my countrymen and fellow patriots, "Nothing but a bunch of AIDS-infested faggots."

Boy howdy. Now, *that's* polite.

The guy was a drug dealer, and drugs are certainly a scourge destroying our nation's youth, as G.B. put it. Take me and Shelly. If she hadn't been a speed freak, she'd be alive today, and I wouldn't be a convicted felon. Probably. To say nothing of our nation's talented elderly. Russki was a prime example. If it hadn't been for me reining him in now and then, our few remaining Empire chairs would have disappeared up his nose by spring 1990.

But in the end, after a number of atrocities, G.B. showed Manuel up, but good. In his cell he only has one color TV. "Tennis at eleven, tea at three," as M.A.N. POW put it that first year in Miami. If it costs American taxpayers $360,000 a year to keep him in racquets, so be it. I hope they'd do the same for me.

On New Year's Eve, limping around the house with a half-empty bottle of Beefeater in my hand and a purple streamer trailing from my foot, I came to the realization that I had taken my beating from Lee Ann and company lying down. Not only in the literal sense—although, yes, I had indeed cowered like a dog in the dirt while they set upon me—but also figuratively.

I stumbled down to the basement, toasted my G.B. effigy, and made a daring resolution: "Justice will be mine." I planned to launch an Operation Just Cause of my own.

It was not, needless to say, going to be easy. It would have to be a cautious and well-managed Strategic Defense Initiative, bringing to bear the skills I had amassed in the arenas of covert action, psy-ops, and—through constantly having to ferret out Russell's little tricks before they found me—miscellaneous hardware and gadgetry. Lee Ann had had a legitimate gripe with me, but it was downright back-handed the way she'd gotten the others to gang up. I figured I would punish her similarly, by using deception and dishonesty.

The sheriff's deputy would be the simplest adversary, due to the civic and moral standards he was—perhaps unjustly—held to as an upstanding member of the law-enforcement community. I had met him once socially before the parking-lot incident, at the funeral for Lee Ann's DUI/DOA husband. He was fond of football trading cards and liked to talk proudly about his favorite canary, which he had hatched out of the egg himself under a heat lamp. He made an avocation of it, raising chicks by the dozens and selling them to pet stores. Though legally entitled to carry a gun on behalf of the county, he appeared to be a half-wit. I bore him the least ill will of the three.

He had not wielded the pipe himself, although he did assist by holding down my legs while Lee Ann was force-feeding me the products of America's tobacco industry. But even at that moment, from what I could see over Lee Ann's ample shoulders clad in a Def Leppard T-shirt, his face betrayed anxiety and confusion. He was a pawn in the struggle. God only knows what filthy lies Lee Ann had told him about me.

I laid in a supply of specialized tools from Russell's catalogs. These included a midpriced voice-modifying telephone device, a set of lock-picking implements and an exhaustive though poorly written instruction manual, and, from a black-market source in South Carolina Russell recommended enthusiastically to me, a small treasure trove of bargain-basement plastic explosives. This last item was in no way intended for use on the challenged deputy; in fact, I had no plans for the explosives at all. I just ordered them because I could, under Russell's name.

Late one Monday night while it was raining, I purloined half of Russell's stash. I then called up the sheriff's station to make sure Zeb was on the job. I knew he lived alone with the canaries: even at the funeral reception, pimpled chin liberally greased with KFC debris, he had been prospecting clumsily for romance. I still recall his sadly ineffectual pickup line, used on a voluptuous teenage girl with glinting orthodontics as she loitered over the coleslaw while he scavenged through the pile of deep-fried chicken parts for drumsticks: "Do you like songbirds?"

I donned dark clothes and gloves, leaving Russki in a trance in the bathtub, and headed through the rain to Zeb's apartment, where I broke in successfully without leaving any marks on the lock. I was grateful, as I executed this graceful maneuver, for the fact that we live in a free country, where supply and demand are unhampered by the State. There were no vehicles or signs of human life in the vicinity; I passed the birdcages and heat lamps and went straight to the bathroom, where I stowed the powder, encased in Ziploc, in his toilet tank.

This done, I made an anonymous voice-modified phone call and in one fell swoop crippled poor Zeb's credibility. His suspension was not covered in the newspaper, of course, but I heard about it through the grapevine at the factory. Pending a full IA investigation, Zeb was on a long vacation.

A complication arose when Russell discovered the discrepancy. I had overlooked, in my otherwise careful calculations, the fervor with which he monitored his coke supply. I told him I had used the cocaine myself, on a low-energy day, in an attempt to bolster my productivity at the workplace. He was enraged, but when I handed him one of my paychecks in compensation and promised to behave myself in future, he softened his stance somewhat and allowed me to make it up to him with a few undignified activities.

Lee Ann's brother-in-law was a more difficult target. He was a car salesman who enjoyed some good repute among the churchgoing set and had given generously to local charities such as the John Birch Society. Also, he was venomous as a cottonmouth and twice as vicious. I could not attack him physically; nor could I attack his credibility in the retail community. Rather, my strategy had to be intelligence-based and aimed at subverting his loyalty to Lee Ann. She'd used him to get back at me, and now I had to turn the tables.

I recalled, from the long-lost days of our workers' solidarity, several pieces of key information she had conveyed to me. Let this be a lesson to all my fellow members of the G.P.: the workplace gossip inspired by daily proximity is a priceless commodity. The canny American employee will accept it readily, even hungrily, but will never give it out for free.

On a slow day over the conveyor belt, Lee Ann had related to me a number of facts. Fact 1: Shortly after her brother-in-law's marriage to a horse-faced but wealthy debutante from Dallas, said brother-in-law had actually proposed to Lee Ann's younger sister, a fulsome peroxide-blond beauty, that they engage in sexual complicity. Fact 2: This sister, Deborah, had acquiesced initially, but finally, overcome by guilt induced by a sermon on Family Values and Fidelity, had brought an end to the arrangement. For weeks the brother-in-law had courted her in an attempt to win her favors back, gifting her with flowers and kitchen-ware to no avail. Fact 3: The debutante had single-handedly bankrolled her husband's business venture, which we'd all since come to know as Jimmy T.'s All-American Cadillac-Oldsmobile. Fact 4: Jimmy T. and his wife did not have an "open" relationship, being Baptists by creed.

Knowledge is the source of all power.

I had in my possession one Christmas card from Lee Ann, on which three Smurfs in yuletide dress frolicked gaily. (I recognized Papa Smurf and Smurfette, but the third celebrant was unknown to me.) Inside the card there was a sample of her ungainly handwriting. As a further aid to mimicry, I had a recipe for homemade hair-removal cream she'd written out for me, inscribed across the top

ESPESHULLY GOOD FOR ARMPITS. This almost brought a tear to my eye. It had been the zenith of our Camaraderie.

But I steeled myself, recalled how I had gagged on the Menthols, which I can't smoke to this day, and repeated my resolution firmly.

For anyone with manual dexterity, forging is candy from a baby. Time and close study are required, but no artistic genius. So my next move, in what I was calling Operation Just Because, was to write a letter to Jimmy T.'s wife. In it, I described with quiet restraint her husband's extramarital misdeeds. As an insurance policy, I warned her that I would never speak of this again: I had already betrayed my sister once because I loved the truth, but from this day on my lips were sealed. I thought she had a right to know, being, myself, a God-fearing woman; and seeing her sitting dutifully beside her cheating husband every Sunday in the pew tore at my Moral Fiber. But I was not involved and could take no further responsibility. If she loved Jesus, she would not—ever—approach me for clarification. If my sister knew I'd leaked the family secret, she would always hate me. "And anyway, all that I know," I wrote, "I've told you in this letter. Praise Be."

I signed it Lee Ann, wiped it clean of prints, and mailed it with a flourish.

Two days later, I donned a fake beard and gray sweat suit and began to stake out the ranch-style Jimmy T. domicile with Russell's high-powered binoculars, which he usually used to watch the younger neighbors in their bedrooms. Jimmy T.'s curtains were always closed. Unfortunately, my reconnaissance was limited to those hours in which I was not gainfully employed; it took me almost a week of observation, before work in the morning, after work at night, plus weekends, to determine the lay of the land. I hardly had time to see Russell at all and had to miss my daily policy discussions with G.B. I was reaching the end of my tether when victory finally came.

At 8 A.M. on a Saturday, a pickup truck pulled up to the driveway and parked. The driver got out, wiped his hands on his pants, and rang the doorbell. Out the front door came Jimmy T., struggling to heft a stack of boxes manfully. Atop the pile, teetering in front of Jimmy T.'s scowling face, was an old high-school trophy.

Jimmy had been a wrestler in his glory days.

Anyway, I knew Jimmy T.—if only by reputation and via the end of a blunt instrument—and I suspected he was not the type to go gently into that good night. No: he would rage, rage against the dying of the light. He would pinpoint the culprit in short order, I was sure. I expected to hear that Lee Ann had had her car tires slashed, or maybe even her windshield smashed with a large rock.

So I congratulated myself on a successful indirect strike.

But actually it turned out she had moved to Calgary two days before, to work in a rodeo. Jimmy T. put his car dealership to the arsonist's torch after his wife filed for divorce, collected the insurance money without a hitch through some John Birch Society friends in the claims-adjustment business, and left town with a beautiful underage, mute stripper. The deputy retired voluntarily from his work for the county before they even finished the investigation and went into bird-breeding full-time. By early March, I heard he was doing a solid business in rare subtropical species.

And then, one morning on a Saturday, I saw him at the library in the next county. He was showing his birds to a group of children, giving a talk on their migration and mating habits in the wild, and imitating their songs. I caught sight of him from the periodicals table, where I was sitting scanning the major newspapers for items on G.B. Various birds perched on his shoulders, feathery bodies green, blue, and red. He looked like a challenged Saint Francis of Assisi.

I walked past him on my way to the counter to check out my books, and he suddenly smiled and waved at me. I was caught off guard and didn't know what else to do, so I waved back.

I puzzled over his happy smile and carefree wave for half an hour, while I was driving home. All I could come up with was that he recognized my face vaguely, but couldn't quite place me.

1990

1. Maggie

We're not discussing intervention. I'm not contemplating such action.
—PRESIDENT GEORGE BUSH, August 2, 1990

This will not stand. This will not stand, this aggression against Kuwait.
—PRESIDENT GEORGE BUSH, August 5, 1990

A few minor historical events took place in the early months of 1990—I recall G.B. signing the Americans with Disabilities Act with two wheelchair guys sitting there on either side of him, and then there was the upcoming German reunification, which unrolled largely without the hands-on engagement of G.B.—but that was the calm before the storm, for both him and me.

By late summer, while G.B. was preserving post–Cold War global harmony by talking Comrade Gorbachev out of genociding some Lithuanian rebels, I was making frequent trips to the hospital to visit Russell, who'd suffered a heart attack. I'd found him on the couch when I came home from work one day, apparently asleep, with his baggie and razor blade beside him on the coffee table and an AARP magazine open facedown on his lap. He wouldn't wake up when I shook him, so I carried him to my car and drove him to the ER, where they gave me a tongue-lashing about "letting" a geriatric do cocaine. As if Russki kowtowed to me.

They insisted on keeping him under observation for ten days to monitor his EKG, then moved him to a clinic to "wean" him off his "chemical dependency." Three nights a week, I had to join him in a low-ceilinged room with fluorescent lights where they served coffee and stale wafer cookies, for group family therapy. I certainly did not enjoy the sessions, which consisted largely of Russell haranguing me in front of everyone for not agreeing to smuggle in his stuff. The arguments were useless, since all I did was tell him they wouldn't let me in the place if I was carrying. They checked all bags as visitors went in. But Russell felt we should explore the potential of body cavities. I disagreed.

On one occasion, a teenage girl with multiple facial piercings broke into tears, clutching a ragged teddy bear with safety pins for eyes as she delivered a scathing indictment of her own personality. While she was being embraced by her crying frizzy-haired mother, and both of them were being patted on the back by the dependence counselor, Russell became impatient. He hurled his half-full cup of decaf onto the floor and stepped up onto his chair with trembling difficulty; I grabbed him around the waist to steady him. Then he cleared his throat—Russell had a powerfully repulsive cough, like the sputter of a lawn mower encountering pebbles—and began to speak.

"Rivers and mountains, we're all dirt to me. Heh! Dirt we are and dirt we shall remain. A rush is all there is. You can't give it to me. Do I got places to be? Nowhere. You stupid slut. And neither do you. There are no goals. Aims, goals, objectives, shut your face."

At this point he swayed, and I had to tighten my hold on him. But then he started up again, bicycling his arms in the air as I struggled to keep him from toppling. The teddybear teen stopped crying and started blowing her nose, and other families stood up and headed for the cookie table on a spontaneous coffee break, which usually happened when Russki went on a rant. The frizzy-haired mother stood there glaring at him like he was a stain on the carpet; the dependence counselor tied her shoelaces twice in a row and tried to ignore his insults. Russell particularly disliked her. "You wouldn't know yourself from a hole in the wall and I tell you what, there's hardly any difference. All tiny men. Tiny, stupid, and pointless. Ignorant slut."

I thought it was strangely poetic and wrote it down when I got home. But I don't remember the rest, because Russell soon swayed and fell off the chair, pinning me beneath him and then rolling off and breaking his hip in the process. He screamed in pain and finally got the attention he deserved.

Luckily, no one had understood the speech but me, due to the distortion of the voice box. One of them whispered that Russell sounded like static on the radio. But it was the most I'd ever heard him say, and I appreciated the eloquence. Russell was a philosopher.

And I have to say, that sermon brought him closer to me. In physics class, when Shelly and I were in tenth grade, the teacher used to show us movies of mushroom clouds on a regular basis, to demonstrate the importance of Science. Two of the wimpier girls in our class made a suicide pact after viewing a reel called "Aftermath of Nagasaki." They slit their wrists in the locker room, having composed a joint suicide note that said the world was evil. They spelled it E-V U-L, actually. They were found before they even lost consciousness; the cuts weren't deep and they were given codeine by the school nurse. (Typical of the L.B.: they couldn't spell and they didn't die, but they still got better treatment than me or Shelly.)

Still, their parents threatened litigation and got the physics teacher fired. It made an imprint on Shelly. Not the suicide pact; both the girls were cheerleaders, and she'd beaten up one of them twice for calling me a pachyderm in

Biology. But Mr. Lee convinced us both. He'd been trying to show us the awesome power of the Human Mind, was what he testified to the Board of Education. Instead he taught us at an early age that no matter what we did, we were already fucked.

But we appreciated his good intentions. And we were pissed that he got fired; you could see the same stuff on TV. So Shelly funneled Nair into one of the cheerleaders' shampoo bottles, and she lost a big tuft of blond hair over her right ear.

What I'm saying in a roundabout way is, I could see Russell's point re: the futility of life in all its forms. Still, you do what you can. And if, like me, you were one of the thousand points of light in G.B.'s Samaritan industry, you had to keep your house in order. Before all else come faith and family. So I was there for Russ whenever he needed me. Realizing that he would require constant care when he got home, I moved in wholesale. During his hip surgery, I removed the last of my belongings from the trailer and scoured and scrubbed to make sure the security deposit would be duly returned to me.

A woman should not remain alone too long, however. We are frail Flowers. And even when those of my gender are not physically delicate, we tend to be needy in other arenas. Near the beginning of Russell's second hospital stay, I had noticed one of the new loaders at the plant shooting suggestive looks at me. His name was José Jimenez, and he spoke no English. My Spanish, sadly, is also limited. The only words I know are shower-room slang I learned in Min, and not appropriate for getting-to-know-you conversations.

In spite of the suggestive looks and gestures, I wasn't instantly convinced of his affections. I am not presumptuous, for I have noticed that many gentlemen tend to be intimidated by me. It may be the combination of my powerful stature with my sharp, often belittling wit and sagacity.

But when, sitting across from me at the cafeteria table,

José put down the fork with which he had been shoveling meat loaf into his hungry maw, hunched down against the table edge, and slipped both hands between my thighs, I felt I could reasonably conclude that he was well disposed toward me. In his country, I reflected pensively as I twirled my own fork amid congealed macaroni, they have an appreciation for the Rubenesque physique; and perhaps, south of the border, straightforwardness is common, too.

I led José out of the factory that night and drove him to the house. We did not speak, lacking the tools, but were able nonetheless to comprehend each other. Although I did not possess the physical advantage I had grown accustomed to with Russ, since José was fully able to lift imported cars by their fenders, my IQ clearly had José's beat by a factor of at least three. And with the additional leverage afforded by the fact that I knew all the customs of José's adopted land and could maneuver well linguistically, I did not expect José to exert an undue influence on me.

Indeed, he was grateful just to have a peaked roof over his head, as he had been residing for several months in a corrugated metal shack on the outskirts of a low-level toxic-waste facility. This I learned from one of the Hispanic gals who worked in Quality Assurance and acted as our interpreter on breaks.

As his English improved, through the picture books I brought him from the library and under my tutelage, I became familiar with the details of his background and history. He was married—twice, in fact—and sent much of his slim paycheck to one or the other of his wives, who lived in two separate slums in Mexico City with two broods of urchins whose precise number he could not estimate. He was an illegal alien, paid under the table at the rate of three dollars an hour. I knew G.B. would not approve of this, but on the other hand José was excellent protection in Russell's absence, and G.B. would surely have made an exception in the cause of preserving a patriotic citizen's safety.

Like me, José had not always been well understood by the authorities in his native country. Based on what he told me, via charades, about the quality of life in Mexican prisons, the ones I'd known began to look a bit like Greenwich, CT. José had had a tough couple of years, and I was willing to cut him some slack where his lack of gray cells was concerned.

Anyway, he and I were eating BBQ ribs side by side on dead Sarah's Louis Seize love seat when CNN broke the news about Iraq invading Kuwait. Now, at that time we didn't know—and when I say "we," I mean the American people, on whose behalf, like G.B., I sometimes take the liberty of speaking—that Saddam was the reincarnation of Der Fuehrer. Those of us who read the newspapers were under the impression that Iraq was an ally, more or less. They bought a ton of our grain-belt produce. As the U.S. ambassador in Baghdad told Saddam two weeks before the invasion, politely expressing our official policy, "We have no opinion on the Arab-Arab conflicts, like your border disagreement with Kuwait."

Plus which, as everyone knows now, Kuwait was basically a feudal monarchy, though it was hard to tell at the time. The Emir had hired an American PR team that was paid to bandy about the term *democracy*.

So José and I went on eating our ribs. He spilled large dollops of A.1 on the priceless love seat, which I made him clean up, and later we played a game he liked called Dos Perros. José was very open-minded—you might even say impressionable. Because he didn't know the culture, he was prone to take suggestions seriously. For instance, I'd acquired the habit of carrying around a wallet-sized and well-thumbed picture of G.B. Whenever he came on TV, I would slip the snapshot out of my pocket and kiss it. I can't explain this, except to say that it was part of a ritual I'd developed, to show my respect for G.B. and promote a friendly intimacy. Well, after the first three nights of this, with me and José watching from the love seat, G.B. appeared, patrician and elegant as per usual, on the tube. And whoops-a-daisy, José whipped out his own picture and kissed it just like me. He was matter-of-fact about it, as if it were mandatory. Turned out he'd cut a color photo out of a magazine and had it laminated; I guess he thought G.B.'s portrait was like the Pope's ring.

That was fine in the home, but one night we went barhopping with some of the other loaders, and I have to say that when G.B. came on the screen over the bar, and José pulled out his glossy and gave it the tongue, some of them stared at him. He didn't even notice, although from then on they treated him differently. I think he assumed everyone else did it, too, as a display of patriotic pride. Poor José was a trouper.

On August 2, before G.B. flew off to Aspen to speak with Maggie Thatcher at a conference, he told reporters the U.S. wasn't considering butting in. So there again, it was business as usual for José and me. I spoke to one of the hospital nurses on the phone, and she said Russell was on morphine for his hip pain, and happy as a clam. José and I ate our Hungry Men and played Dos Perros in the Jacuzzi.

But then, when G.B. got back to DC on August 5, he made his play as soon as he alighted from Marine Corps One. He was afire with Righteous Passion, which burned in him like a cold flame. When he said with his trademark Firm Resolve, "This will not stand!" everything changed for me, in the turn of an instant.

That very moment, I fell in love for the first time. G.B. had spent his life as a Boy Scout till then, standing knock-kneed at the end of a line with his fingers raised in the Scout salute. Waiting to lead the charge of the Light Brigade. And like a Middle Eastern scoutmaster, S.H. had blown the whistle; G.B. could do his duty now and earn his merit badge. For a place in History. His pale eyes lit up above his knotted neckerchief, full of delight. I recognized his face at once, where I hadn't before. He was the shy boy with the stutter: I'd known him long ago, when I was young.

I sat upright in my seat, leaning forward a little. I caught my breath. I saw the sun of G.B.'s Presidency rising over the horizon, casting a soft morning light across the fields and gray buildings of the cities. I saw the orange rays of Manifest Destiny hitting church spires and bathing the bodies of pedestrians like me, as, crossing the street upon our daily rounds, we glanced up to the east and glimpsed the globe of the new day low in the sky. I felt uplifted by the vision of our common future, borne aloft on the rising breeze of a great crusade.

I saw it. And it was beautiful.

I got up from the sofa, leaving José behind, and went upstairs and onto the roof with my bottle of gin. I sat on the tar paper for a while and drank, my skin humming like there was friction in the night air, goose bumps rising on my legs. Then I got up and paced, as the trees bowed and rustled around me. I was grappling with my recognition. It was no longer platonic between G.B. and me, but it wasn't mundane either. I've always been the practical type, but there was Spirit filling me and reaching out with warm arms. I told myself I had to stay grounded, batten down the hatches, steer a steady course. But I was soaring like a phoenix, out of the humdrum ashes. And G.B. was soaring, too. He stood in his gray-and-green kneesocks and shorts before a vast army, and he was as lonely as he had ever been.

We would be lonely together.

I finished my bottle, cried a little at the tragic majesty of the sentiment as the rain began to fall, and went back downstairs again.

And when I saw José's broad, swarthy countenance atop his thick neck, large-pored and not a little greasy from the rotisserie chicken we'd been eating, his sleepy, bloodshot eyes dulled from the infusion of pure lard into his intestinal tract, it was not a happy comparison. That night I turned out the bedside lamp the second we lay down, right before our combined weights suddenly broke the bedsprings and sent the mattress slumping to the floor.

I decided then that I had to change my ways and try to be pure.

Because I needed to be alone with G.B., I started to leave José at the plant at the end of the working day, claiming I had girlfriends and godchildren to see. It was unfortunate that this left him with no place to call home save the three-walled shack on the dump site, but I cannot be my immigrant's keeper.

José got a hangdog look the fourth night I drove off without him. I would have given him a lift—it was a three-mile walk to the CAUTION HAZARDOUS MATERIALS sign that served as his welcome mat—but that might have led to a slumber party, which would have sullied me. I sometimes have to rein in my native generosity. So, to tide him over, I offered him two slabs of processed cheese food in a slice of Wonder bread that I hadn't eaten at lunch, smiled and waved cheerily, gunned the engine, and was on my way. It just couldn't be helped. I had matters of state on my mind.

The English, with their snobbish superiority, were claiming all the credit for G.B.'s policy turnaround on Iraq for their Prime Minister. One of their newspapers said M.T. had performed a "backbone transplant" on G.B. out there in Colorado. It's typical; these minor island states want to believe they're pulling all the strings to make us Yankees dance. The way I see it, we're just sorry for the English, which explains our chronic leniency.

Since M.T.'s piddling economy had vested interests in Kuwait, their former protectorate from when the Empire still had balls, M.T. was acting bossy. "We will fight on the beaches," etc. Although she didn't have the plumbing, she deluded herself that she was the modern W.C. The English had sold a large amount of military equipment to the

Emir's family and even hung around in the capital to show the filthy-rich morons how to use it.

But I say this: M.T. had no more of a relationship with the Emir than G.B. After all, when G.B. was still an oilman, his company, Zapata Offshore, had drilled the first-ever off-shore well in Kuwait. And that was recent history, unlike the failed colonial gambit.

From all accounts, in any case, it was a pretty intimate weekend G.B. spent with M.T. I wondered idly how B.B. felt about it, until I realized that M.T. is a man if ever there was one. And G.B. is not an ardent supporter of the Love That Dare Not Speak Its Name.

So I wasn't too jealous.

Over the next week, as the escalation began, I needed to spend all of my weekday nights with G.B. He talked with King Hussein of Jordan and promised to give the King time to find an "Arab solution" to the occupation. But he broke that promise after his tête-à-tête with Maggie. And G.B., whose word is pretty much his bond, was obviously feeling guilty on that score, which I detected with my intuitive ESP. At the same time M.T. was laying the groundwork for a Protestant Jihad against S.H. by telling the press that he exemplified "the evil in human nature." Her approval rating at home was 24 percent at the time, the lowest in English history, and soon she would resign. She was singing her swan song.

Of course, the L.B. media was whining on and on about how we hadn't heard those colorful phrases when Libya invaded Chad; China, Tibet; or Indonesia, East Timor. They harped on about how just eight months before G.B. had ordered OJC, in flagrant and breathless violation of the Panama Canal Treaty. It was typical of the L.B. They've always confused economics with morality.

It was time America stood up for the Emirs of the free world. And I couldn't have been one iota prouder of President 41. Take no prisoners, G.B.

I'd started to tape CNN during the day, while my role as a stalwart blue-collar American worker kept me away from my duties to G.B. At night I would fast-forward through the tape during commercials in the live coverage, until I caught sight of him. And then I'd sit there dreamily, a deer in the headlights of his transformation. G.B. was a man of action, a G.I. Joe fresh off the assembly line with special-edition gray hair. Only like those Russian dolls, there was a different G.B. inside the warlike Commander in Chief: a gangly prepubescent. The tension between them transfixed me. It was like his voice had changed suddenly, while he was giving a presentation to his Scout troop to earn his Shotgun Shooting badge. All he'd had before was Bugling, Dog Care, Rabbit Raising, and Insect Study. I heard the high-pitched squeak, and my heart broke for him.

I was watching him closely the evening of August 8— the day he announced the imminent deployment of U.S. troops—when I was rudely interrupted. José had walked about fifteen miles from the factory to turn up on my doorstep. It was pouring, and he was soaked.

I opened the door, albeit reluctantly. I was extremely irritated. Under duress, my charitable view of José was quickly caving in. You can only restrain your critical faculties so long for the sake of a warm body. And when I saw him standing there, his yellowed Salvation Army workshirt plastered to his all-too-abundant flesh, shivering in the downpour with blue lips, the patent absurdity of the relationship became obvious to me. There was a widening gulf between us. But I let him in and we played what only I knew was our final game of Dos Perros.

The next morning I put in a discreet call to the Department of Justice. I told you I had a mean streak; I can take a firm hand when need be. Anyway, I didn't think it was doing José much good to be homesteading in radioactivity.

Poor José was deported the day G.B. ordered the first fifty thousand troops to active duty. (Our President had been sternly warned by Maggie, "George, this is not the time to go wobbly.") They picked up José at the factory and, as we found out the next week, slapped a mammoth fine on the backs of my esteemed corporate employers. I regret that small regulatory intrusion, but the step I'd taken was strictly necessary. I'll never forget how, as the INS van pulled away, José looked out at me from the bed of the truck and, one last time, slowly and humbly kissed his laminated picture of G.B.

He was a fine patriot, I willingly concede, but too high-maintenance for me. Russell was due home from the hospital, finally, and I had my relationship with G.B. to think about. I had to stay abreast of new developments in public policy, and that takes hard work. Half a league, half a league, half a league onward, into the valley of death rode the hundreds of thousands. Led by G.B. and observed avidly by me.

2. Desert Shield

The mission of our troops is wholly defensive . . . they will not initiate hostilities.

—PRESIDENT GEORGE BUSH,
press conference, August 9, 1990, scripted speech

I think it is beyond the defense of Saudi Arabia. So I think it's beyond that.

—PRESIDENT GEORGE BUSH,
press conference, August 9, 1990, Q&A

My Boy Scout in the White House knew where he was going from the start. He had consulted his pocket compass, and the needle was quivering between "War Powers Resolution" and "First Strike."

It was an auspicious and exciting time, what with the large-scale mobilization of our troops, by mid-September costing taxpayers about $29 million a day. A bargain. You can't put a price tag on glory. Everyone and his brother felt downright historic; it had the momentous panache of an impending WWIII. We were an empire again, and it was scoring 75 percent approval ratings for G.B. He had been Born Again in the opinion polls, and I was watching his ascent there somewhat fearfully. Because we were still living in hungry Reaganite country; my fellow Americans would line up behind G.B. only as long as he stalked like a predator, slavered at the chops, and pretended to wipe his drooling fangs on a sleeve.

Russell had a new synthetic hipbone and had been prescribed a couple of months' worth of Percocet, so he felt he was sitting pretty. He lay on the sofa all the time in front of the TV, which forced me to use the second, smaller TV upstairs for my sessions with G.B. That was working out fine, until one night there was a realignment in our domestic geometry.

I'd stopped on my way home to buy a goodwill present for Russki in the form of twelve Original Glazed Krispy Kreme donuts. Russell had virtually no appetite, so I looked forward to the pleasure of consuming the lion's share myself. Imagine my shocked chagrin when, green-and-white box in hand, I entered my base of operations and saw that he had company.

Russell's complete lack of friends, or even casual acquaintances, had long been a selling point for me. His isolation from a larger community was both liberating and complimentary. To find him lying in the living room with his legs up on the sofa arm and his teeth on an end table, sharing visibly stiff whiskeys with what appeared to be an Appalachian mountain man, was unnerving to say the least.

The mountain man had a matted, gray beard that hung almost to his waist. I would not have been surprised to find small animals nesting in it. He was wearing a safari jacket of Lawrence of Arabia vintage, which apparently had not been doused with water since the turn of the century. He committed his first faux pas right off the bat, in what was to prove a defining moment for me. When I came into the room and was standing staring at them at a loss for words, he jerked a thumb in my direction and asked of Russell, "Who's the roly-poly?"

And then he proceeded to eat eight of the donuts himself. Little did he know, at that instant, that he had made his worst enemy.

The mountain man turned out to be an old comrade-in-arms from Russell's service days. Or postservice, to be precise. After leaving our nation's armed forces in the wake of their separate Korean experiences, they had met in the VA hospital, got along famously, and subsequently worked together for over a decade as soldiers-for-hire, that is to say, mercenaries. It was a part of Russell's life that, until then, he hadn't shared with me, and I found it hard to believe at first. I guess I'd had some preconceptions about mercenaries. We all have our prejudices.

Anyway, our visitor went by the unlikely name of Apache and now, in his dotage, made his living as a part-time truck driver. His eighteen-wheeler was parked down the street, illegally. I was not pleased to be informed that he visited Russell annually and was planning to stay for a week.

Leaving them to while away their time by telling tired anecdotes of senseless brutality, I made my way to the basement and locked the door to my private chamber. This done, I repaired to the kitchen to cook them a three-course meal while developing my strategy quietly. I had quickly determined that I would work, over the first couple of days, to enlarge Apache's trust in me by playing the part of the servile domestic female.

In those months I was walking a tightrope both at home and at work, where I had started angling for a ten-cents-an-hour pay raise. I was cannily maneuvering to optimize my personal freedom and my opportunities, in steadfast pursuit of the Founding Fathers' bright dream.

Apache seemed to be opening up to me by the third night, when I barbecued steaks; he tore into his sirloin ravenously, as I sat beside Russell and diced his portion into small pieces, and made several grunting noises that I interpreted favorably. But the next day, when I came in at 6 P.M., Russki was dozing splay-legged on the bathroom floor and there were eight empty Red Hook beer bottles beside the Louis Seize. Russell looked down on beer as a weakling's drink; I knew there was only one possible culprit. Sure enough, Apache, drunk, stoned, and wandering through the house, had picked the basement lock. I came upon him standing in front of my G.B. media crucifix, leafing through my most recent policy memo file, a homegrown joint dangling from the side of his chapped mouth.

"Lady, you're fat and you're freakin' crazy," he drawled, crassly but not unaffectionately.

"This will not stand," I said, taking a hint from G.B. and clenching my jaw. "Put that down and get out of here."

"Eat me," said Apache.

An energetic struggle ensued. I was taken off guard by his strength and agility; the hirsute old codger had lightning reflexes and evident martial-arts expertise. I soon realized I had made a grave error of judgment in engaging him in combat physically. Ten minutes after hostilities had been initiated, the sour-smelling carpet of his facial hair was flowing over my face, blinding me, suffocating me, and tickling my nostrils unpleasantly, and my wrists were pinned to the floor while Apache had his way with me.

I was not new to the game, fortunately—on the contrary, I was by that time a seasoned veteran—and was able to relax eventually, to minimize abrasion. When Apache slunk away, I had only two bracelets of bruises to show for my trouble, plus an incipient kidney infection and a small cut above my left eyebrow.

What does not kill us makes us stronger, and I came out of the episode extremely Firm in my Resolve. That night at supper, a tacit social understanding seemed to arise between Apache and me. So long as I did not bring up the subject of his rude Assault with Russell, he wouldn't mention his basement discoveries. (Personally I'm not sure Russ would have minded what Apache had done to me; he wasn't the jealous type, and he wasn't what you would call "overprotective" of me. I've never had an "overprotective" boyfriend, come to think of it. You don't see gerbils guarding a warthog.) We ate Tater Tots and spaghetti in sullen silence, with Russki breaking the silence occasionally to reminisce about a boyish escapade the two of them had shared in Angola.

But Apache's behavior really rankled me. I'd had a lot of that in Max, and I figured I'd exceeded my quota. Plus which, I had been trying to steer clear of entanglements that dirtied me. The episode was disrespectful of G.B.

After the meal I retired to the empty guest bedroom that contained the second TV and while eating ice cream watched taped footage of President 41 until I fell asleep. I considered approaching the authorities with reference to Apache, but dismissed the notion, deciding such action would be bound to have unpleasant repercussions ultimately. I had broken my parole the year before, by relocating to take the job at the factory. (My parole officer had found only sewage work for me, and the fumes had been sparking blackouts that reminded me of those olden days on PCP.) So red tape was one of my many enemies.

With only three days remaining in Apache's planned visit, I had almost decided to let bygones be bygones when he announced to Russell and me that he was extending his vacation.

The truth of the matter is that I could not identify Apache's Achilles' heel. Every man has a weakness, and every woman, too; and it is never wise to launch a first strike without foreknowledge of the target's vulnerability. And because of the détente that had arisen between us, I had few chances for in-depth study. No matter how many meals I cooked him, I could not win over Apache to induce him to confide in me. Like G.B., I cannot be all things to all people; some of my fellow humans lack the ability to see the greatness and the wistfulness in me. Frankly, I will not stoop to teach them.

"The anchor in our world today is freedom," G.B. had said in his 1990 State of the Union. I didn't know about that metaphor at the time. If I had been G.B., I would have found myself some new speechwriters. Correct me if I'm wrong, but I'm under the distinct impression that an anchor, like a leg shackle, is there to hold us down.

Still, the sentiment was nice, and fully worthy of G.B. When he talks about freedom—and he does, he used the word *free* twenty-one times in that State of the Union address—he means it. That was becoming clear to me in the early days of what they were then calling the Persian Gulf Crisis. The thing about freedom is that the more you have, the more the next guy doesn't. It's kind of like fresh water: as long as you're upstream, there's plenty to go around. The freer you are in the mountains, the thirstier they get near the sea.

Take Max Sec, for example. If I exercised my freedom to defend myself against bodily assault, that meant that Rump lost her freedom to express sexual preference. Either way you sliced it, someone wasn't free.

And there could be no freedom for me while Apache the mountain man was ruling our roost. The sight of his beard over the breakfast table, its greasy tendrils decorated with fragments of scrambled egg, made me nauseous for an entire day as I recalled our forced intimacy. I ceased to cook for Russell and him, and I regretted that I had not yet learned how to rig up a simple incendiary device. One would have fitted snugly beneath his truck's right front wheel.

I was between a rock and a hard place. There were only so many hours I could spend on the factory floor. I tried passing the time at local bars, but I was growing highly impatient to be back, safely ensconced and media-vigilant, in my personal war room dedicated to G.B.

As Week Three of Apache's stay began, I was set in an uncomfortable routine. I would put in an hour or so of unpaid overtime at work, making sure, when possible, that my supervisor saw me; eat a microwaved dinner in the employee lounge, which resembled nothing so much as a WWII bunker; and return to the house via Skullduggery, the nearest purveyor of liquor and entertainment, around ten, when I usually found Russell and Apache snoring in their armchairs amidst empty beer and whiskey bottles, a pornographic videotape playing on the TV screen. I would then sequester myself for the rest of my waking hours in the guest bedroom with G.B.

In the midst of a tortuous budget struggle, he had courageously vetoed a minor civil-rights bill that didn't meet his high standards of legislative excellence: the Civil Rights Act of 1990. Congress impudently tried to override the veto, but their override fell one vote short, 66–34, and they were feeling impotent compared to G.B. Plus, G.B. had reluctantly given the rubber stamp to a couple of "revenue increases," incurring the wrath of the fiscal-minded GOP. Sure, he had reneged on his tax pledge, which simplistic pundits said had gotten him elected; that didn't matter to me. It was the posturing manliness of the phrase *Read my lips* that had first interested me in G.B., not the apparent substance of the no-new-taxes message. Fiscal policy is for the small-minded, for the cheap hoarders among us who begrudge the poor a buck or two of Earned Income Credit. It has never been my interest or my specialty.

Anyway, G.B. fell into a temporary public-approval tailspin—from which he would soon recover dramatically, like the true fighter pilot he used to be—and, isolated from the peons of his party, was flailing weakly. I watched him day after day on the televised campaign trail for the upcoming Congressional elections, and more than once I winced. Every sting to G.B. pierced my thin skin just as deeply. At a campaign rally for a Republican candidate in Vermont, G.B. was lambasted by said candidate right up there on the podium. Even though our generous forty-first President had deigned to sit beside him in a gesture of support, Rep. Peter Smith, a freshman Congressman running for reelection, said extremely rudely, "My specific disagreements with this Administration are a matter of public record."

When G.B. got up to speak, he was so hurt and confused all he could say was, "We have a sluggish economy out there nationally. That's one of the reasons I favor this deficit so much."

And then he went off on the hostage situation. Even though the U.S. ambassador in Kuwait City had said that the diplomats had plenty of food, G.B. charged they were "being starved by a brutal dictator." At another campaign rally in New England, he went on to say that Iraq had "committed outrageous acts of barbarism. Brutality—I don't believe that Adolf Hitler ever participated in anything of that nature."

G.B. was committing senseless gaffes left and right; he was a raging bull in a china shop. Although I felt for him, I was also worried. G.B. was supposed to be a steely pillar of strength for me.

With Week Four of Planet Apache, the leaves were falling from the trees and my frustration reached a fever pitch. I missed my personal space; I missed the pre-Apache peace and harmony. I was nervous and antsy. So on Congressional Elections Day, which brought in a poor to mediocre showing for G.B. and company, I visited a doctor—something I had not done since the lead-pipe incident due to the costs involved—and complained of insomnia. My hysterical tears, and the dark rings beneath my eyes, convinced the doctor that my claim was honest, and she prescribed powerful soporifics.

At home I ground several of these into a powder in the bathroom, using dead Sarah's stoneware mortar and pestle, and packed the powder into a straw with tape on both ends. On the pretext of wishing to clear away the thirty-odd beer bottles that had accumulated around Apache's nest in front of the TV, I circulated amongst the debris and scouted out the scene. He was apparently drinking from a tumbler he had placed without a coaster on the Chippendale end table Russell had had appraised at $10,000. When he slouched out of the room to answer the call of nature, and Russell's half-open eyes were trained on the semiclad body of a hermaphrodite on Adult Pay-Per-View—no doubt a product of the sheerest artifice—I slipped the straw from my pocket and emptied it into Apache's libation.

Half an hour later both he and Russell were sleeping like babies. I took advantage of the respite to make an exhaustive search of Apache's belongings, which he kept in a ragged Army Surplus duffel bag. There were threadbare undershirts; unclean socks with holes in their heels; an old towel; a pack of playing cards; a loaded and locked Glock semiautomatic; a utility knife; a T-shirt emblazoned with the legend *So what if I farted?;* an unused stick of Old Spice deodorant; chewing tobacco; Q-Tips in a less than pristine condition; and at long last, at the very bottom, a slim dimestore photograph album.

I opened it and flipped through the pages. The album contained pictures of only one person: a blond girl. The earliest snapshots featured her around the age of three; the most recent, in my estimation, around the age of fourteen. Always thorough, I slipped each one out of its casing, searching for a clue to her identity. The closest I came was a childish scrawl that read *Love U Daddy.*

After carefully restuffing the bag, I moved next to his safari jacket, which hung beside him on the arm of the chair. He had taken to walking around the house barechested, allowing a full view of his pocked and scarred torso. (One nipple had been lopped off in the Crimea.) I knelt down and stealthily searched the pockets. His wallet, to my delight, held an additional picture of his daughter. On the back it said *Chrissy.*

I was still lacking vital information. I took his keys and went outside and down the block to the truck. In the glove compartment I found a dog-eared address book. There was no Chrissy listed under his last name, but since there were only four people, total, in the address book, I had no trouble singling her out. Under the *P*s I found one address labeled simply *C*, with a telephone number in Louisiana. When I called the number and asked for Chrissy, the woman on the other end said, "She's asleep, whaddaya think? And who the fuck are you to call this late?"

I ad-libbed and said I was Apache's girlfriend.

"Yeah? You tell that mofucker to stay the hell away from Chrissy and me."

The next day, around the time that my lunch hour began, Apache received a call from a nurse at a Baton Rouge hospital. Chrissy was very, very ill and was asking for him. Her mother had told the nurse not to call, but she was so moved by Chrissy's plea that she had taken matters into her own hands. Given the urgency.

According to Russell, who told me about it drowsily when I got home with a brand-new box of Krispy Kremes, Apache had peeled out before three.

3. Chickenhawks

A majority . . . rejects some of the Bush Administration's main justifications for military action: protecting oil, defending Saudi Arabia, and expelling Iraq from Kuwait. But a majority does seem convinced that stopping President Hussein's potential to build and launch nuclear missiles is a valid reason to take action.

> —Results of *New York Times*/CBS poll,
> reported November 20, 1990

Every day that passes brings Saddam Hussein closer to realizing his goal of a nuclear weapons arsenal.

> —PRESIDENT GEORGE BUSH, November 22, 1990

We could face an Iraq armed with nuclear weapons.

> —BRENT SCOWCROFT, National Security Adviser,
> November 25, 1990, on *This Week with David Brinkley*

It's only a matter of time before he acquires nuclear weapons.

> —RICHARD CHENEY, Secretary of Defense,
> November 25, 1990, on *Face the Nation*

G.B.'s best buddies in the White House—Quayle, Cheney, and that ugly mug Sununu—were dubbed "chickenhawks" by the smarter-than-thou bourgeois press. This term referred to their Vietnam draft-dodging records combined with extreme bellicosity as engineers of G.B.'s foreign policy, and although normally I don't like to take any cues from the L.B., I thought the tag was apt. I didn't trust those guys as far as I could throw them. In other words, not one inch further than ten feet.

Plus there were the real hawks, like Scowcroft. I strongly suspected they were just using G.B. The White House wasn't consulting with any real Middle East experts during the escalation, so the chickenhawks could say what they liked and G.B., because he has a trusting manner when dealing with fellow Republicans, would listen. And as soon as they read in the *Times* that nukes were the only way to scare the American public into a war mood again, they started playing that card like it was the Ace of Spades.

Because by early November, the war ardor of my compatriots had cooled. Reality had begun to set in, and the chickenhawks had to flap their wings to fan the flames. They made the talk-show rounds, and everyone was seeing mushroom clouds. It was a red herring, since Saddam's nuclear capacity was five to ten years down the road and we didn't have a long-term plan anyway. But it worked.

I have to admit there was a touch of petty envy in my attitude toward appointees like Cheney. Because let's face it: I'm every bit as qualified to be Secretary of Defense as D.C. And so are you, more than likely. At least I went through college; I didn't like it much, except for the fun I had with Shelly, but I finish what I start. Cheney, on the other hand, whiled away his time in graduate school, copping not one, not two, but seven successive college deferments from the army and then not even bothering to get his degree. G.B.'s loyalty to his friends was admirable, but I sometimes thought he'd gone fishing for them in a stagnant pool. I mean, what separates me from the leaders of this great country isn't character or mental acuity. I feel just as entitled to make snap decisions that affect the General Public as they do. And when I'm threatened, I take the same approach to defense, too: there are a lot of people in this world, and the way I see it, none of the others are me.

It's a logic we all have to resort to when our backs are to the wall, but for the chickenhawks it was more than logic. It was theology.

No, what separates them from me is history. And at times, I admit, I resent that.

I'd slyly sold an ugly china shepherdess statuette that Russell had never noticed by sending it off for auction to Sotheby's in September. With the proceeds, I was able to settle my medical debts and buy myself a new wide-screen TV with a surround-sound speaker system and VCR for my war room. When, a couple of days after the elections, G.B. had announced from the White House briefing room that he was sending an additional 150,000 troops to Saudi Arabia—over 350,000 had been ordered over there by November 11—I was sitting alone watching it.

I observed the deployment announcement again and again, as close to the TV as I could be without the images melting into grainy color fields. There were no windows in the basement: it was a dark, warm cave that contained only me and G.B. My new monitor's vast, flat screen was constructed of a soft material that dented at a touch. It was almost as though I could step through the thin fabric into the source of the light itself—and come out next to G.B. The space between us was practically intangible. And I realized G.B. was on the path to recovery from his postbudget, preelection illness.

I daydreamed a lot while I was on the assembly line at the factory. There wasn't anyone to talk to. Lee Ann had been replaced by a high-school dropout who disappeared after five months, and then by a deaf lady named Hayley, who was led around the factory floor on her first day with a sign-language social worker and introduced to everyone. It was the star treatment, so that the supervisor could show off how nice the corporation was to those with disabilities. While I was in the rest room washing my hands, I heard her asking the social worker, from a toilet stall, "She's really good. Have you got any more?"

Hayley hadn't even started her shift yet.

Since Hayley was deaf and kept herself to herself, I was

left to meditate in silence as I folded the box tops and waited for the next crate to be shuttled along to me. Most days I filled the empty, repetitive hours with idle fantasies. I was deliberate in my construction of scenarios; I laid the logistical groundwork carefully before I launched into my flights of fancy. The fantasies ranged from the slapstick to the sentimental and were all set within or after G.B.'s second term. By then, when he had safely been reelected and was guaranteed his birthright, I figured he would be able to dismiss any adverse publicity that might arise pursuant to our union. Short of impeachment, Congress, the pundits, and the GOP would then wield no weapons against him, and he would be free to pursue an alliance with me.

In an early scenario G.B., like Edward VIII, who followed his heart and forfeited the throne to marry Mrs. Simpson, would claim new statesmanlike territory as the first President to eject a First Lady from the White House forcibly. In my more whimsical moods, I liked to plan the occasion. For instance, I saw myself presiding discreetly over the separation proceedings, languidly sipping a spiked ice tea with a slice of lime on a White House balcony. G.B. and I were watching as B.B., bent over nearly double with the effort of trundling an ugly Vuitton suitcase behind her on a collapsible frame, made her way down to the curb and a waiting taxi. When she reached the curb, she slipped on a small dog patty. As she slid yelping to the ground, G.B. did not even flinch. Instead, he stood straight and proud, with a gentle hand on my shoulder, beside me.

That one made me feel guilty, so I shelved it and tried again. This time, B.B. left the Casa Blanca (as José had called it) of her own accord, with no knowledge of the tension and longing between her husband and me. She waited until after G.B.'s reelection, then revealed that she had decided to leave the country of her birth forever, to spearhead a dynamic new Crusade Against Illiteracy in Sierra Leone. Amid the off-key blowing of trumpets she stepped onto a private jet, which whooshed her away to the far-flung West African jungle. And there she lived in peace and near-total obscurity for the rest of her days, except for an occasional grainy black-and-white photo in the back pages of *People* or *US,* which showed her in safari gear, reading *Uncle Tom's Cabin* to a group of half-naked children in the shade of a thatched hut.

Divorce was widely deemed unnecessary, and I became G.B.'s "close personal friend." I fired all his advisers politely but firmly and accompanied him to state dinners and public speaking engagements. Partners in diplomacy, we jetted across the globe together. Once, several years later, we happened to be in the capital city of Sierra Leone, where we had flown on a high-profile UN peacekeeping mission. We were sitting at a long table on a restaurant terrace, overlooking the bright, shimmering sea, with parasols above us and sparkling water at our elbows, when we glanced over at the dusty town square. And there we saw, straddling the broad back of a pack mule, B.B.

She was wearing a sun visor and overalls, and a dab of white sunscreen on her nose; she'd ridden into town to pick up a shipment of *Little Womens* and some penicillin. G.B. called out, "Hey, Barb!" and she waved at him cheerfully but dimly, with a faint, maternal smile, and then kicked the mule, which plodded slowly away.

And in a third tableau, I took the initiative personally, announcing her replacement by me at a televised press conference from the White House briefing room. "My fellow Americans," I said, wiping a tear from the corner of my eye. "This is a love story. It is also the story of our country—of war, freedom, and pageantry; of hardship, conquest, and yes, adultery. But I would ask you not to judge the President or me harshly, lest ye be judged harshly yourselves. Even while we fall to our knees and ask for your forgiveness, America, we know that our souls are drenched in the virtue of a sacred honesty. We could not lie to you about our love.

We hereby inaugurate a new epoch in this nation's proud and pioneering history, in which public servants will no longer lie baldly but will open their mouths and admit to their failings and their humanity. My fellow Americans, the truth shall set you free."

Afterward, resentful but also dumbstruck, in a daze of strange reverence at my oratory, the adulterous millions would murmur perplexedly in their homes, sleep on it, and awake suddenly illuminated by the sunlight of common sense, to a dawn in which hypocrisy had been banished.

Unfortunately, these narratives bore little resemblance to my home life. Sure, Russell had let up on the larger-scale pranks after his hip surgery. Since then he'd only played one joke on me, and it was halfhearted: a box of straight pins in my cornflakes. Physical intimacy was as alien to both of us, by then, as childhood innocence. But that was fine with me, since from the outset it had been a losing proposition. He moved more slowly and painfully now, and some days he chose not to rise from bed at all. And instead of growing fonder of me as I fed him and tended to his bodily necessities, he was becoming increasingly ill-tempered and mean. When his Percocet supply ran out, he switched from yuppie cocaine to crack, and day turned to night in terms of Russell's personality.

One evening in the kitchen he snuck up on me with a tire iron, which he could barely lift, and hit me in the side. As I turned toward him in shock and agony, he then bent down and hit me a second time, in the knee. You could have knocked me over with a feather. I was that surprised.

Of course, the attack was a laughable tactical error on his part. I may be a female, but I'm no fragile B.B. Weighing in as I do well over the 250-pound mark, and trained in unarmed combat while deprived of spatial mobility by the judiciary, I can slap down your average feeble cottontop with my right hand while agitating a Jiffy Pop over a burner with my left. Which is precisely what came to pass on this particular occasion. It was pure self-defense.

When I'd stowed the tire iron in a place known only to me, I picked him up and carried him to the sofa. I laid a cool compress over his forehead, and when he came to, I plied him with a hot toddy. It turned out Russell suspected me of stealing his drugs. His mind was muddled, and he was having flashbacks to the occasion where I'd filched his other stuff to set up Francis of Assisi. I gave him a talking-to about Respect and Loyalty, and he listened absentmindedly while scratching at a scab on his elbow, but it was clear to me that Russell was no longer the man he used to be. He was losing his memory and his sense of time, and starting to act randomly.

The next day I received my first letter from the White House. It was boilerplate courtesy. "President Bush thanks you for your vote of confidence," etc.

And I became angry at G.B.

Because by then I felt I'd been influencing policy from behind the scenes for over a year, with my numerous well-researched and sophisticated memoranda. I wasn't asking for public credit, but I at least deserved some recognition from him personally. Even a quickly jotted card would have been sufficient, like the Thanksgiving note he reputedly wrote to Ollie North in '85: "Your dedication and tireless work on the hostage thing, with Central America, really gave me great cause for pride in you and thanks. Get some turkey, George Bush." I wasn't asking for a binding prenuptial agreement. All I wanted was a show of fraternal familiarity. I knew decorum wouldn't let him go further than that.

Although I don't normally like to disclose my episodes of weakness, knowing, as G.B. does, that revealing my human frailty may undermine the popular opinion of me, I have to own I threw a minor temper tantrum. I hammered a nail into the cotton eyeball of my effigy. I tore up my only baby picture of G.B. and burned it over a votive candle.

But that didn't help, so I stepped outside into the fresher air, clutching the fragments of the form letter. It was as though my frontal lobe was being pricked with thumb-tacks, and light blue flowers sprouted behind my eyes when I closed them. For a fleeting instant I surmised that there were spiders in my head.

Fists clenched, grinding my teeth, I strode across my lawn and out into the street, where I hurled the fragments onto a sewage grate. I then got into the Plymouth and drove at high speed toward the highway, startling a decrepit old crossing guard—who tripped as he fled and fetched up against a telephone pole—and scattering a crowd of adolescent skateboarders into a cul-de-sac. I kept a heavy foot on the gas until the steam of rage had evaporated from me, terrorizing a minivan containing an Asian family, which skidded onto an unpaved shoulder panicked by my tailgating.

When I got back to the war room, I fired off an angry—yes, even threatening—letter to G.B. In the heat of the moment, it seemed necessary to vent my feelings honestly. I told him off for letting the chickenhawks run the country. Later, with a half bottle of Beefeater under my belt, I also sent a warning to B.B. in the guise of writing, as a slow-witted child, to her ugly pooch Millie. "My dog is very big and mean. I don't think he would like Millie. I think that he would bite her in the neck and blood would spurt." Or words to that effect. I enclosed a photo of a rabid Dober-man. (All I got back in response to the latter was, several weeks later, a greeting card printed with a color picture of B.B. and Millie and signed with a pawprint.)

I would come to regret these gestures by the early weeks of December. In my own defense, I can only say that freedom of speech has long been one of our great nation's top priorities.

But in the meantime, my anger dissipated. I quickly reforged the bond of my empathy with G.B. I had to remind myself of the rules of executive propriety. His hands were tied by the rigid decorum of his office, clearly. But in no way did this regrettable circumstance point to a lack of confidence in me. And furthermore he was distracted—understandably—by the looming prospect of Armageddon.

I put the form letter behind me and devoted myself, during those evenings in which Russell was calm and comatose and I was therefore not forced to stay on guard against unforeseen attacks, to contemplation of the future.

In the middle of November, fifty-four Dems in Congress filed a lawsuit to compel G.B. to obey the Constitution and ask them first if we could go to war. D.C. scoffed at their paper roadblock; I saw him on *Meet the Press* on November 18. "Congress is a great debating society," he said. "I'm not sure it is the kind of place that is capable of making this kind of decision."

I said, "Ever hear of the Constitution, Dickie?"

The chickenhawks had decided to launch a preemptive strike—against the legislative branch.

4. Joint Resolutions

Bush and Baker [were] nervous about growing opposition to the possibility of war, both in Congress and on the part of the public. They therefore decided to try for a new UN resolution explicitly authorizing the use of force.
—BESCHLOSS AND TALBOT, *At the Highest Levels*

Baker himself presided as president of the Security Council as it convened on the evening of November 29 . . . when the Yemeni foreign minister voted no, applause could be heard from some onlookers in the gallery. Angry, Baker scrawled a note. . . . It read, "That is the most expensive vote you have ever cast."
—*U.S. News and World Report,*
Triumph Without Victory

They won the vote 12–2, with the People's Republic of China abstaining, giving S.H. a January 15 deadline to get the hell out of Dodge. And G.B. reported to the nation on the UN use-of-force resolution the very next day. "We're in the Gulf because of the brutality of Saddam Hussein," he said, pronouncing S.H.'s name wrong as usual. I read later that when you say the name the way G.B. did, accenting the first syllable, it means "Little Boy Who Cleans the Shoes of Old Men." On which the CIA had cleverly counseled him. Psy-ops again.

You sly bird, G.B. And here we thought it was the Texan in you talking.

By late November, G.B. was beginning to soar again in the polls, and Congress was pretty much a parliament of yes-men. As they would prove definitively, under their own steam, in January. By that time G.B. and Baker had worked so hard on international rabble-rousing that Congressional leaders couldn't pull back on the reins.

My love for G.B. was unconditional in those days, much like the surrender terms he offered magnanimously to Saddam. And though I was roiling underneath at the chicken-hawks' manipulation of him, I had to admit that his offer to S.H. to send his foreign minister to DC was a masterstroke of warmongering diplomacy.

"To go the extra mile for peace, I will issue an invitation to Foreign Minister Tariq Aziz to come to Washington . . . to meet with me." No way was G.B. open to discussion; after calling S.H. the second Fuehrer umpteen times over, he couldn't have bargained even if he'd wanted to. It would've looked wimpy. He was hedging his bets, shifting the blame for war to S.H. It was one of G.B.'s finest hours.

But it was not one of mine. For on the anniversary of Pearl Harbor, I was detained by the local P.D., who claimed they were "acting in cooperation" with Department of Treasury and Department of Justice authorities.

I will not soon forget the curious and oddly gratified faces of my coworkers as they grouped around me on the factory floor in a semicircle, like onlookers at the site of a roadkill. They watched in a state of smug satisfaction, chatting in hushed voices among themselves, as the cop sergeant patted me down and stuffed me in the backseat of the squad car. It was the most noteworthy event to take place at the factory since I was beaten up by Lee Ann and company—an occurrence I later learned had been observed by no fewer than eight fellow employees, who'd spectated the assault from behind the snack machine.

In particular, I recall the sharp, pink-lipsticked mouths of the hags in Quality Assurance, who hadn't liked me too much since José's deportation, giggling and whispering behind their scrawny hands.

I hadn't expected the Secret Service to take my hastily

penned words literally, and I was sure they'd failed to have their orders authorized before the fact by G.B.

I was kept in the local jail for only two days, and my incarceration failed to result in an arraignment. During the first night, I shared a cell with an ancient Native American wino who told me right off the bat that he had hoisted the U.S. flag at Iwo Jima. I called him on it instantly, for I have long been a staunch aficionado of the ballads of Johnny Cash. "That was Ira Hayes," I retorted. "He is long dead. You lie like a cheap rug."

Subsequently he revised his story, claiming to be Ira's nephew. It was all in the family, he said. We struck up an acquaintance and settled into a comfortable companionship. He regaled me with tales of the rez, and I told him stories of Max Sec.

But then, during the night, he suffered from some sort of diabetic stroke. I couldn't attract the attention of the sergeant on duty, who was listening to a football game on his Sony Walkman. I spent the night hunkered down over his prone form, holding his head in my lap and massaging his temples, afraid that he was dying. It wasn't till morning, when the duty sergeant woke up, that I succeeded in raising the alarm. They carted him off to the hospital.

And then, throughout my second day, I was subjected to a battery of asinine psych evaluations, which I treated with the contempt they deserved. The P.D. shrink was an atrociously underqualified practitioner interning with the department, straight from state college and barely out of her undergraduate sorority. She had the temerity to ask me, "Where does your anger come from? Is it a self-esteem problem? Do you hate your body?"

I wanted to slap her slim, tanned face into the twenty-first century, but instead replied succinctly, "No, girlie, I hate yours." She was far too dim-witted to understand the retort, merely twirling her blond hair around a pencil, nodding and smiling vacantly. I saw her write on her foolscap pad, in fat, cute letters, *Hostility*. If I had really been a threat to national security, she wouldn't have had a clue. She'd have let Lee Harvey Oswald off with a prescription for Xanax.

I was finally released with a casual remark from the red neck detective, who said the Feds had "bigger fish to fry."

The debacle had two unfortunate repercussions. First, I didn't get the pay raise I'd been bucking for. In fact, I lost my status as a factory employee. Although the informal arrest did not constitute grounds for termination, the company had checked up on me after I was hauled off. When I came back, they argued that I had willfully falsified my original job application, and then they fired me. Specifically, they charged that I had omitted to check the box marked *Yes* under *Have you ever been convicted of a felony?* A trick question if ever there was one.

In short, they got me on a technicality.

The second adverse effect of my run-in with our painfully mismanaged federal-state-local bureaucracy was that, in the course of executing their search warrant, the fascist cavalry had wreaked havoc on my war room. They artlessly dismembered my effigy, which I had to reconstruct painfully; tampered with my files; impounded Russell's service weapon, to his considerable annoyance, which was then directed at me; and stole my computer-generated target of D.C. No doubt for their own private use with their CIA buddies back in Langley. I had designed the target painstakingly on my supervisor's computer, by sneaking into her office at night, and I was aggrieved at the loss.

They did not, luckily, come upon my plastic explosives cache, which was lodged in a mass of urea-formaldehyde insulation in a hole in the bathroom tiles that I had sealed with caulking.

The net result was a temporary loss to the American workforce. On the other hand, the blow to my finances was softened by the knowledge that G.B. had interceded on my behalf, which constituted the first tangible proof I had received of his high regard for me.

Because when I'd gone home for lunch on that fateful day and been told by Russki that the cops had burst in brandishing a search warrant and looking for me, I had instantly written a letter to G.B. In it I acknowledged I had authored the previous note in a passing fit of pique; I apologized for my unruly outburst and pleaded for Presidential leniency. I stopped by a FedEx box and sent it off on my way back to the plant, where the ham-handed foot servants of the law were waiting for me.

So when I was released from custody abruptly, with no explanation save that there were bigger fish in the sea, the possibility of his intercession dawned on me in an Epiphany. I walked out of that Podunk jail with a spring in my step; the birds sang in the two trees remaining on our main street, and they were singing for G.B. and me.

It was a coup, communications-wise. For some time, to circumvent the bureaucracy of the White House mailroom, I had been sending my personal letters to G.B. in care of the Bessemer Trust Company, which handled his taxes and retained power of attorney. I got the address off his FY89 1040, made available for public scrutiny, which listed his and B.B.'s occupations as respectively *President* and *Housewife*. Most of these letters were returned unopened, but a few were not, particularly once I began sticking typed address labels onto the envelopes and stamping their upper left-hand corner with the return address of the General Accounting Office, in a fair simulacrum of the genuine article. I had estimated that there was a remote but nonzero statistical probability that one of the letters would eventually slip through the filters, cross the Oval Office desk, and catch the eye of G.B. or a sympathetic aide. And my quick release suggested this hypothesis had proved valid.

That same day, December 9, S.H. released the first 325 of his First World detainees. It was probably a dumb move for his country, since G.B. would have had a lot more trouble selling the bombing of Baghdad at home while it was full of thousands of U.S. citizens. But it was a straight-up thing to do, and personally I gave Saddam kudos.

I should have been euphoric, frankly. S.H. had handed G.B. a safe and secure place in the history books. But instead I was still wracked with anxiety. The recent spate of injuries inflicted against my person, however erroneously, were sticking in my craw. I would be sitting in the war room watching G.B. fly all over the globe to shore up support for war among the members of his allied coalition, and the disparity between our two stations in life would grate on me. I mean, I wasn't blind to the facts. Because although, in a way, we were soul mates, an outsider would have made the point that I was an unemployed factory worker, while G.B., even on slow golfing weekends, was practicing world domination. But that was exactly the point. Opposites do attract; I'd always felt there was a kind of molecular-level strength in the polar opposition of G.B. and me. Like protons and electrons, or something.

The emotional fallout from the trauma was exacerbated by the fact that there was no longer enough room in the house for both Russki and me. It had been one thing when I worked full-time, but now we were both at home 24-seven, and the wear and tear of taking care of him was starting to show on me. Monday, Wednesday, and Friday mornings I drove down to the state employment agency to browse through grossly exploitative job offerings; Tuesday afternoons I had to take him to his dealer's hovel downtown and wait in the car while he hobbled inside to make his trade. At all other times we were in spitting distance of each other, and Russell sometimes took advantage of that. Literally.

Increasingly he was non compos mentis, afloat in the wide seas of waking sleep. Russell was daydreaming his placid way into the illusion of unconscious race memory.

Except on Tuesdays, when he stayed sober from breakfast until afternoon for the purpose of conducting business, he was a lesson in inactivity. He was a passive resister to life itself; he was becoming his own memory. He was the memory of himself, slowly dissolving into the air.

However, be it ever so humble, his very presence in my general vicinity was starting to annoy me.

He spent most of his time in the living room and in the bathroom, where he apparently enjoyed lying in the bathtub, in first hot, then tepid, and finally cold water. I often had to barge in and pull him out, shivering violently. Russ's small suite was of little interest to me, but I did spend a fair amount of time in the kitchen, which led directly to the living room, where he watched TV. With Christmas fast approaching, I felt I deserved a yuletide gift from me. So I decided to test the Russki's perceptivity by first closing and barring, then blocking off, the door between him and me. True, he no longer had easy access to the kitchen; but he didn't eat snacks and he could always enter the long way if need be. The arrangement worked well: for hours at a time, between the meals I served him and my daily collection of his waste products and laundry, I was able to ignore Russell entirely. He didn't seem to mind the plastered-in door; he probably figured it had gotten brittle like his bones, aging along with him. I realized the separation was effective when on Christmas Eve morning, wandering through the house in search of an errant bottle of gin, I tripped over something bulky and inert and had to regain my footing by grabbing on to a sideboard. Sure enough, it was Russ, lying curled on the dining room carpet in the fetal position. In his hand was clutched a festive kazoo.

He may have thought it was already New Year's Eve. In any case, I checked his pulse efficiently; found it, as usual, faint but rock-steady; and continued about my own business. That holiday week, odd as it may seem, was the one in which I procured what I took to be promising gainful employment. There was an opening for a dishwasher and loading-unloading adept at a large diner-style restaurant at the mall, an establishment that catered to the geriatric set. The rate of pay was less than ideal, but I have always loved to be among other people, and I felt that the food-service industry could be an excellent venue for my communication skills. Plus which the physical setting for my work—the mall itself—represented the high point of our American culture in the late twentieth century. There capital cavorted in its myriad fascinating forms, and the middle class strolled aimlessly, simply spending their surplus and waiting for something to happen. In such proximity I would have numerous opportunities for advancement, and might even be able to move laterally in the retail industry.

My day on the job was quite a disappointment. When the first of my new coworkers approached me, another dishwasher-dogsbody, I found her admirably friendly. I was glad that my restaurateur bosses had decided to heed G.B.'s advice and reach out to the needy. But scarcely half an hour had passed before I noticed that, of all those employed in my own line of work and other closely related taskings, numbering a total of five kitchen workers, I was the only one not afflicted with Down's syndrome. I left the premises rapidly. Yes, I wished them all well and fervently hope that to this day they are scrubbing, loading, and rinsing happily, but as you may well imagine, it was an insult to my intellectual dignity.

Over the Christmas holidays, G.B. stayed at Camp David. He was more and more sure, as he celebrated the birth of the Savior out there in nature, burdened only by the presence of his family, that he was doing the right thing. I learned later that during that time he said, "I've got it boiled down very clearly to good versus evil." Way to go, G.B.

Russell, on the other hand, was beyond good and evil. As I had expected, he hadn't even noticed the passing of

Christmas, and on New Year's Eve, while S.H. was giving his soldiers a pep talk in Kuwait, there were no kisses and streamers for Russell and me. Instead, I packed up some rare Dresden china painstakingly, sitting on the floor in front of my wide-screen TV, for another shipment to Sotheby's. My funds were low, since the income stream had been dammed by the beavers of industry.

Russell had just sold the Louis Seize, a little the worse for wear after Apache's slovenly sojourn, but still worth more than I had earned the previous year. He had made his biggest antique haul to date, so he was in the pink, with a larger supply than usual of his narcotic of choice. I was confident that he could not have cared less about the loss of eight table settings and a few oversize tureens.

I checked in on him fifteen minutes before the ball dropped in Times Square and noticed nothing out of the ordinary save for the fact that he was frothing at the mouth.

"Russki," I said, squatting on the carpet to shake him roughly by the shoulder. "How's it going? You fine?"

At first he said nothing, merely drooling with his eyes rolling back in his head.

"Russell," I insisted. "You doing okay, buddy?"

"The dogs of war are nipping me," he rasped. At least that was what it sounded like.

"Listen, big guy," I said. "Before I leave you lying here, I want to make sure you're enjoying yourself. Are you under the weather or anything? Or is it business as usual again?"

"Rotten apples," he muttered. "Infamy."

"Happy New Year." I gave him a chaste kiss on his bald spot and patted him kindly before returning to the countdown.

As it turned out, "infamy" was the last word he ever said to me. When I came back upstairs to check on him again half an hour later, after the clock had struck midnight and the crowds had roared out their battle cry to the future, my poor Russell had finally—and maybe blessedly, though I don't want to go out on a limb here—OD'd.

I washed his face and carried him to his bed, where I dressed him in his plaid dressing gown. (He didn't own a suit.) With a single candle burning, I read aloud his speech from group therapy as a private eulogy. I was guilt-ridden that I hadn't been there when he went. Although, to be honest, I'm not sure he would have appreciated it much. But I slept on the floor at the end of the bed anyway, in penance.

It was hard, and I had nightmares. In one of them I was Lee Harvey Oswald, abandoned by the powers that be. I found myself standing over the bulky corpse of B.B. with a sniper rifle in my right hand. Her double string of pearls had broken off her turkey-wattle neck and I was gagging on it; pearls filled my throat and I couldn't speak up in my own defense. And then G.B.'s disembodied head appeared floating in midair beside a shoe, silent except for the rustle of static, and its tongue stuck out and waggled obscenely. Behind it the Joint Chiefs of Staff jogged on the spot and picked their noses.

They were naked as jaybirds.

In the early morning I woke up parched and went to the kitchen to pour myself a glass of water. I tried to sleep in my own bed, but only tossed and turned. So I got up and I padded back to Russell's room, looked down at him, held his wrist for a minute, and then lay down on the floor again, this time with a pillow. And I had yet another bad dream.

This time G.B. and Russell were one man with two faces. I was beside G.B. on a bus, and he was wearing the ratty plaid dressing gown and carrying Russki's crack pipe. I tried to grab him, to take it away, but then he turned to get off and I saw that the back of his head was Russell's face.

1991

1. Deadline

George Bush trusts very few people . . . he's been listening to other heads of state, but I don't think he has reached out very much to the expert community.

    —*Newsweek* correspondent, *Frontline*, January 15, 1991

I watched G.B.'s interview with David Frost on January 2. I'd been at the mortuary all afternoon, and I was exhausted. The funeral director had argued with me for a good fifteen minutes about the color of Russell's funeral suit: he was pushing for powder blue over a ruffled shirt, which I felt would make Russell's corpse look like a Las Vegas bridegroom. Then he tried to sell me a five-star coffin that would last till A.D. 6000, withstanding even nuclear blasts; and the only cemetery plot they had available at a reasonable price bordered a concrete wall next to the interstate, with a billboard looming overhead.

I opted for cremation. At that point he started pressuring me to hire some kind of curly-haired choirboy from the local Baptist church to sing at the ceremony, so I decided to forgo the public "viewing" of the deceased altogether. The vista wasn't real scenic, and as far as I knew, no one was coming anyway. I splurged on the urn, though, selecting cast bronze over the basic sheet-metal box. I told them not to burn the false teeth; I didn't want the ashes to contain things Russell had hated. The funeral director nodded disapprovingly. His attitude irked me, so I told him not to let them burn the voice box either, because Russell had hated that, too. He pinched his lips together, but said they would respect my wishes. Finally I thought of the disk in Russell's knee, which had given him twinges constantly, and told the funeral director they might as well send me anything that didn't burn or melt instantly. He practically spat on me.

As a result of all this, I had a mood hangover. I was feeling grouchy and depressed during the David Frost special and even got impatient while they interviewed G.B. and B.B. together in the Roosevelt Room. Usually I watched the First Family like a hawk, but when B.B. started waxing less than eloquent about the beneficial effects of prayer, my mind started to wander; I ambled into the kitchen and poured myself a snifter of brandy. And I went so far as to snicker when G.B. said, "Family, faith, one nation under God—I mean there doesn't seem to be much cynicism about all that."

There were times, even at the height of my rapport with G.B., when I almost suspected he was stupid.

Russell's memorial service lasted all of ten minutes and consisted of a senile minister hunched over a lectern garnished with a pot of lilies, reading from a dog-eared prayer book and coughing. Mr. Stims had been our next-door neighbor before he was moved to a home; he was also a Man of the Cloth, ordained through the U.S. mail. I was the only bereaved person present besides a rancid-smelling homeless gentleman who had wandered in off the street and spent the whole ceremony scraping purple gum (grape flavor) off the heel of his shoe and weeping piteously. He said he was a vet and went to all funerals for vets in the county.

He laid a small plastic flag on top of Russell's urn, right

after Mr. Stims had coughed one last time and mumbled, "Roswell, may you rest in peace." And when Stims finally tottered out the back of the columbarium, I took the veteran by the arm and steered him to a diner across the street.

In honor of Russell's esteem for servicemen, I treated the veteran to a plate of scrambled eggs and home fries and listened to his grievances about Agent Orange. Later, however, while I was in the bathroom, he drank the syrup straight from the stainless-steel pitcher, which irritated the waitress. She was trying to force him to leave when I got back, insulting him by making reference to his Poor Hygiene. He called her a Whoredog, and she slapped his face. I played friendly mediator and got him out of there; but after we'd parted company a few minutes later, I discovered he'd stolen all the cash from my wallet. Leaving only Russell's obituary, which I'd clipped from the paper.

I had contributed two lines of the text: "He is mourned by his loving common-law wife, Rosemary. Donations may be sent to Rolling Thunder." That was a bikers' organization Russell had mentioned to me, which sponsored an annual ride-a-thon dedicated to the cause of bringing back POWs/MIAs. It had been one of Russki's two or three cherished beliefs that many of our best and brightest young lads had been abandoned in the jungle by king and country and were still suffering needlessly at the hands of the cheeky Viet Cong.

A few days into January the Senate passed its grudging war resolution, which won by a five-vote margin after major lobbying by G.B. He was getting religion in the New Year, before he sent in the bombers. His Episcopalian minister told him to turn the other cheek, so in the end he got his blessing for war from Billy Graham, who's often called upon for spiritual mentoring to Presidents in need. And I began an early spring-cleaning campaign, which mainly involved giving such of Russell's personal possessions as were valueless but still functional to the Salvation Army.

The Army wouldn't take everything, though. Upon discovering that Russell had quit this vale of tears the proud owner of an astoundingly bounteous supply of his narcotic of choice, I took it upon myself, in a gesture of charity that paid tribute to his pragmatic personality, to drive downtown into our small "red-light district" late at night. There I presented the baggie as a gift to a woman I found sleeping in a bundle of rags in an alley. Sure, I didn't approve of drugs myself, but one man's poison is another man's meat, and waste not, want not. Etc.

I was in mourning for Russell, but it wasn't an easy grief. It wasn't simple or straightforward. He'd shrunk into a wraith those last months, and the few times we conversed for longer than a minute, he mentioned death like it was a trip to the bathroom. Russell didn't have much reverence for the invisible line between Consciousness and Oblivion. Six of one, a half dozen of the other, was how he felt about life and death.

I reckon that, in his years as a mercenary, he'd probably seen a lot of people go. He was indifferent, not afraid. And he seldom hesitated to speak ill of the dead—unless, say, the dead had been a soldier killed in the Korean War. You couldn't say a word against a dead soldier to Russki, or he would creep up on you while you were sleeping and drip hot wax on the back of your head until you woke up screaming. I had found that out the hard way.

In a nutshell, the weirdness of his being dead was background noise, and in the foreground was a strange new buoyancy. It was the agitating thrill of being free. Not free from a building—I knew how that was already—but free from captivity. Because the first real estate agent I showed the house to said we could put the asking price at $450,000 quite reasonably. I nodded politely at the figure, with casual restraint, and performed my exuberant dance of prosperity only after she was out the front door. I dashed from one end of the house to the other in great bounds, flapping my arms as though they were the wings of a bird, and jumped up and down crying, "Whoo-hoo-hoo-hoo."

I'd won the lottery. It gives you an airy feeling at first, as if you've stepped off a platform into a space with no ledges or footholds. So I was floating in ether, cruising on an updraft into the stratosphere. I wandered the house in a trancelike state for hours at a time, plotting out my magnificent future without a map. But now and then an object would distract me, like a bill from the Yellow Rose Funeral Home or a rusty mousetrap beneath the basement stairs. And I would feel the prick of guilt and have to anesthetize my conscience with Bombay Sapphire gin.

It wasn't that Russell had died, although he had. It wasn't that Russell had died alone, although that, too, was true. Nearing the end he'd had no use for his fellow humans, and that included Yours Truly. But something nagged at me like a shadow moving out of sync with a body, and I couldn't see it clearly.

I put the house on the market January 7, and a mere two days had passed before my first potential buyers toured the premises. I was asked to vacate the house for an hour, which I spent browsing the aisles of a grocery store. (I worked on teaching myself not to compare cereal prices on a per-ounce basis, automatically.)

According to the Realtor, they were a young couple wishing to start a family. They admired the house, but were dissatisfied, the Realtor revealed to me, with the quality of the local School District. There had been two shootings recently in one of the grade schools in our area. On one well-publicized occasion, a fifth-grader had smuggled a sawed-off shotgun into his locker, bypassing the metal detectors by entering the building through a broken back window, and later ventilated another fifth-grader. They were engaged in a rancorous dispute over a handheld Nintendo. I remembered it clearly, since I had sent the newspaper clipping to G.B. the Education President, with annotated commentary. I figured he might want to keep his finger on the pulse of learning in our nation's public schools.

My next potential buyers that week, fortunately, were not planning on having babies. They had quite a large family already, as the Realtor explained to me, for they were the administrators of a growing religious organization whose "children" were its devotees. The two persons in charge—"Father" and "Mother," as they liked to be called—promoted the teachings of a Santa Fe guru named Hatamishi. But Father and Mother were frugal and would not go higher than 400, which was unacceptable to me.

Throughout the second week of January, I packed and shipped the remainder of Russell's fine antique inventory. This task was often accompanied by delicate, sporadic heart palpitations and a boundless euphoria, not unlike the sensation pirates must have had while running their dirty fingers through piles of gold doubloons. There was regret, but there was also Victory. I divided my time between winding sheets of bubble wrap around table and chair legs and watching CNN religiously as we counted down the days to the war.

On the night the ultimatum ran out, I watched *Frontline* with a cardboard box from the mortuary on my knees. The box had been sitting in the front hall for days. I hadn't wanted to open it. It contained my "keepsake" portion of the ashes, in a wooden bowl with a latch, and the last of Russell's personal effects from the furnace. Each item was balled up in pink tissue paper.

I unwrapped the denture case first and with a shiver of repulsion dumped it into the trash can next to my chair. There was no love lost between me and the teeth. Then I unwrapped the wooden bowl of ashes and set it on the mantelpiece. But there was still a pile of tissue-papered bundles in the bottom of the box, like eggs in a nest. I put it aside for a few minutes and relived the escalation via *Frontline*, which was punctuated by clips of G.B., phrasemaking. The show finished with a narrator pronouncing ponderously, "And so, at the end of the game, the leader of the last super-power seemed to be holding all the cards." It sounded like ad copy for WWIII. At that point I gave up taking notes for the night. It was seeming increasingly pointless.

I drank my Seabreeze through a bendy straw and sat there staring at the screen with the MUTE on. There was kind of a pregame feeling. I thought I caught a glimpse of live footage showing the cities of the world lifting off into the air, moving upward as columns of bright, tingling dust, so I turned the sound on again in a panic. But it was just a commercial for homeowner's insurance. I changed chan-nels, and everywhere there were omens of the end of his-tory. For instance, a cloud of maxipads that turned into butterflies reminded me of departed souls flitting to heaven, leaving behind their worm bodies. When a luxury sedan whipped down a freeway across a stunning desert into the red dusk, $499 a month to lease, all I could see was the test-blast site for Fat Man and Little Boy.

Eventually I clicked off the TV entirely and slid down onto the carpet, where I sat cross-legged and fumbled in the bottom of the box. I pulled out first Russell's metal knee, then a metal bolt from his shin, then part of the arti-ficial hip. Next there was the voice box, charred and twisted, then a handful of shrapnel, and finally something I could not identify that looked like a gray dish.

Drunk as a skunk, I gazed blearily at the artificial parts spread out around me, queen of a human junkyard. The parts made me feel bitter, lasting forever as they did. A jar of pennies was on the coffee table; I reached up, scooped out a bunch, and lobbed them, one by one, at the parts of Russell. My vision was starting to blur. Finally, though, I ran out of pennies. And I was at a loss vis-à-vis entertainment possibilities, so I turned the TV on again. And there was G.B., nodding, saluting someone behind the camera, and smiling his thin-lipped smile as he moved through a crowd of blue and gray business suits. I rubbed the metal plate pensively, and then, in a flash, I saw the forest for the trees.

I'd been dragging myself around the house for two weeks like I'd lost the feeling in my legs, heavy with remorse. Beating myself up. I hadn't cherished Russki; I hadn't appreciated him. How would his mother have felt if she had held him close when he was three months old and seen the old pervert he would become? If she had bounced him on her knee and then seen him seventy-six years later, as he crabbily scratched at his groin and said, "You stupid, stupid slut"? And kicked the neighbor's cat upside the head for sniffing at his crack pipe?

It was just sad.

Point was, whether or not Russell deserved it, I was feeling guilty just for screwing one guy. Meanwhile G.B. had deployed half a million, for the purpose of personal Fulfillment.

That's when I saw it: a President must be insane.

I understood that for the first time on the eve of war in the P.G., and I don't need to tell you it explained a lot. I felt like I'd been in the dark for years, as I climbed up the worn runners on the stairs to my bedroom. And now a gentle light was filtering through.

Knowing G.B. to be unmoored, to be unhitched from the buildings and the blueprints of rationality, to be floating in the blackness of the universe and the whirling colors of the disappearing world without a compass, I burrowed that much more snugly into the covers on my bed. A great weight had been lifted from me, to be honest. If you spend your life acting like Society should make sense, etc., it can give you chronic insomnia and even gastrointestinal distress.

Because if you're going from a faulty assumption off the bat, then nothing quite falls into place. It's just like if you claimed the earth was flat and then tried to explain a sunset. You can bang your head against the wall trying to analyze the complexities. But once you know about the grandeur and the scope of pure insanity, the whys and wherefores get simple.

I'd be lying if I said my revelation didn't change things between me and G.B. It did. But only for the better.

2. The Storm Breaks

We do not seek . . . to punish the Iraqi people for the decisions and policies of their leaders. In addition, we are doing everything possible—and with great success—to minimize collateral damage.

—PRESIDENT GEORGE BUSH, February 1991

The damage shut down most of Iraq's sewage and water treatment plants, leaving the Iraqi people susceptible to the rapid spread of cholera, typhoid, and other diseases. The U.S. Census Bureau's Center for International Research estimated that the poor health conditions contributed to seventy thousand civilian Iraqi deaths after the war.

—*U.S. News and World Report,*
Triumph Without Victory

The war was a roller-coaster ride for me. It was a euphoric time, nervous, frantic—the high point of my relationship with G.B. We were clinched together for the whole six weeks, tight as two sumo wrestlers.

First of all there was the sale of the house, for in late January I hit the jackpot with two spinster sisters and their live-in nurse. Lynn and Margery were infirm physically—Lynn used a walker and Margery had a clubfoot—but powerful financially. They had recently been awarded a large settlement in a lawsuit against a pacemaker manufacturer, whose substandard merchandise had caused the untimely death of a parent. They offered 425 firm, and you can bet that I took it. Meanwhile I was continuing my advocacy with G.B., sending faxes to the Casa Blanca every other day from a citizens' access communications center named Kinko's

Copies. Knowing that G.B. was not a stickler for correct sentence structure, and being under deadline pressure myself, I abandoned the Briefing Memo formula to which I had previously adhered. My faxes increasingly took on a poetic, jubilant tone—an off-the-cuff Joie de Vivre. This I achieved through the copious use of exclamation points, sometimes up to ten in a row.

After the bid on my house came in, I bought my own fax machine and began to communicate regularly with defense experts at the Pentagon. I focused my collaborative efforts on an elite group of combat strategists known in armed-forces circles as the Jedi Knights; they were quite influential in the military-industrial community. You may be surprised to learn that both the northern air campaign from Turkey and the powerful attack of the Twenty-fourth Infantry Division were ideas that originated with me.

On January 25 I saw a clip of G.B., on *Larry King Live,* saying insistently, "I am not going to be held captive in the White House by Saddam Hussein." A few seconds later I wrote him a fax that read simply *NO SIR G.B.!!!!!!!!!*

As the closing approached and I prepared for my imminent move to Washington, DC, I watched the war almost hourly on my square battleground. I delighted in the path that G.B. and I were forging. It was not a new path; it was the dog track of history. I went back and forth on the subject of the advisability of our mission against humanity, but on good days I figured it was everybody's fault for being blind and stupid. "Carnage, terror, big deal," was what I liked to say under my breath to G.B. "It's the animal kingdom." And finally, in this instance the L.B. was not solely to blame; rather, it shared the guilt with the P.B. and the G.P., its natural enemies.

In the End of Mankind we would all be united.

The day our planes dropped bombs on Shelter 25 in Baghdad, killing four hundred people (mostly civilian gals and kids), we showed Steel Nerves in the face of Adversity.

If Cheney had gotten his way, the Casa Blanca might have seen some real public outcry. Because when D.C. heard the news about the civilian casualties, he laid his finger alongside his nose like Santa and told G.B. they should not express compassion.

Luckily for G.B.'s reputation, Marlin Fitzwater disagreed.

Like G.B., I let my behavior grow instinctive and spontaneous. It was an act of solidarity: I went with my urges the way he went with his. And also like G.B., I was always sure to make peaceful, diplomatic overtures before I began hostilities. For instance, when two gum-popping Girl Scouts appeared at my front door and tried to sell me double-chocolate cookies, I sent them packing with a liberating wallop to the smaller one's ear. Before I struck her, however, I attempted honest diplomacy by asking what other kinds of cookies they could offer me. (I was looking for low-fat varieties, specifically.) When they said, "None," I knew that, much like Satan, they were there to tempt me.

As they ran away crying, their braids and skirts flying, the small one dropped three of her boxes of cookies on my walkway. I scanned the street quickly, looking both ways, before descending from my porch, creeping along the path, and surreptitiously kicking the cookie boxes beneath a bush. Under the cover of darkness, I returned and carted them inside, where they were forthwith consumed ravenously.

A subsequent visit paid by the small Girl Scout's father also did nothing to deter or dissuade me. "And who might you be?" I said, opening the door to him clad only in a T-shirt on which I had (in the early months of my fervor) artistically stenciled the words *Hail to the Chief: My Patriotic Hero G.B.* Beneath this legend was his silhouette. The shirt had shrunk in the laundry, though, and did not fully cover my child-bearing hips.

Looking down at me quickly, the father, who was thin and sickly, then averted his bulging eyes and stammered, "Excuse me! I believe you assaulted my daughter."

"Certainly not," I stated firmly. "I merely held the wolves from my door. She was here flogging high-calorie foods and trespassing on my private property. You need to discipline her severely. She was extremely pushy."

"Just stay away from her," he mumbled dispiritedly, and retreated with his tail between his legs.

"Next she'll be selling scag to six-year-olds," I warned him stridently as he made his timid beeline for the sidewalk. "It's a small step from that double-chocolate bullshit. If I were you, I'd keep a sharp eye on her savings account. It may start to mount rapidly."

I carried G.B.'s no-holds-barred attitude into the realm of interpersonal relationships, too. Although it was true that I no longer had to concern myself with the accumulation of wealth, I still bore a healthy animosity toward my supervisor at the factory. Yes, the nature of the labor and the rate of pay had been less than satisfying to me; no, I did not wish to assume my former position on the assembly line again. That would have been ludicrous for someone of my advanced station. But I was still, every so often, jolted by an unpleasant memory.

I still saw, in that lonely time before falling asleep, my coworkers jeering as I toppled sideways into the squad car. I still watched nervously as my supervisor tightened her lips and removed my ratty job application from a vertical file, then pushed it across the gray Formica tabletop and pointed to the empty box beside the typed word *Yes*. And then to the box marked *No*—which did, in fact, contain an *X*.

The disrespect inherent in her attitude sat poorly with me. Neither she nor my coworkers had known me for the person that I truly was; they had underrated me. It was as if, on occasion, I passed a mirror made of their eyes and saw myself reflected as a distortion: a weird, bruised troll with broken teeth looked back at me, then slunk off and hid again beneath a dirty bridge over a river of sludge.

Short of extirpation, there was no sure way of getting rid of the lingering image of the troll, which they had passed on to me. It stuck to my skin like white on rice. I made up my mind to reestablish balance in the hemisphere of my employment history—declare my independence formally before I moved to another part of the country.

How, you may ask? With weaponry. A task like that cannot be accomplished solely by pacifistic means. At least, not rapidly.

I excavated my explosives from their cave behind the bathroom tiles and repaired the damage with plaster and caulking, out of consideration for Lynn and Margery. For ten days of work hard as Boot Camp, I studied, I learned, and I attained a level of expertise I hadn't marshaled previously in the field of plastique. And then one Sunday night at 2 A.M. I headed over to the factory.

A burly Vance security guard was on duty, but he was dozing when I snuck into the lobby through the Employees' Bathroom. His large, grizzled head was facedown on the reception desk beside a half-eaten sausage in a cocoon of wax paper, and a *Happy Days* rerun was playing on his miniature black-and-white TV.

I entered the small administrative compound stealthily; picked the lock on my erstwhile supervisor's office; and rigged the plastique to the bottom of the toilet tank in her private bathroom, beneath her glossy picture of Harrison Ford, clipped from a magazine. Taped to the strike package was my own inspirational photo: G.B.

Half an hour later, from two blocks away, I watched the blooming orange flower of the blast. It was small, but sure enough the roof was flaming toward Orion as I sank my foot onto the gas pedal. Peeling away, I rolled down my window and raised a middle finger in the direction of the factory, chilled and exhilarated at what my native ingenuity could do. If consequences were forgot, nothing was off-limits to either G.B. or me.

I tried not to contemplate the possibility of my vengeful fire catching, ripped by the wind into walls of flame that ate up sausage debris and melted the *Playboy* key chains of dull-faced, sleeping fans of Fonzie. I shrugged it off, for like G.B. I was determined to be fierce. A dog of war, a crazy fox of holy rectitude. An animal doesn't know or care about the future or the past.

At least, that's what I hear.

I felt pretty wild and free for the whole ride home, until I was in my bedroom again. Then I stared at the curtains, turned on the TV in case there was a special news bulletin about the explosion, and ended up watching a docudrama about a housewife with multiple personalities.

But anyway, on that particular occasion my footloose and fancy-free insanity strategy didn't come off quite as well as G.B.'s. On February 15 he was calling for the Iraqis to rise up against S.H., giving the green light to a coup—his sly answer to Radio Baghdad's offer of withdrawal negotiations—while I was being hauled into the sheriff's station and questioned about my whereabouts on the evening of the fire. "There's another way for the bloodshed to stop," said President 41 daringly. "And that is for the Iraqi military and the Iraqi people to take matters into their own hands, to force Saddam Hussein the dictator to step aside."

The damage to the factory's capital assets was minimal, but the guard had been put on probation by Vance for dozing off on duty, and his brother, a loader I used to know, had fingered me as a Disgruntled.

Our new sheriff's deputy was brighter than Zeb, but insecure and a little edgy. I told him in no uncertain terms that there were at least a couple hundred other Disgruntleds like me. For a start, there were the ones who'd been laid off in the latest downsizing. Plus which, I pointed out, I wasn't the sole employee with a record; I recalled a machinist who'd done three and a half in Attica and liked to brag about it. Basically, they had nothing at all on me. Still, the deputy's assignment was to trap a Disgruntled into some kind of half-assed confession, so I spent almost an hour talking to him in the station before I was released. Fortunately for me, he was no expert on criminal psychology. He asked me some subtle questions to suss out if I was an arsonist, such as "Do you like to burn people?"

Since he was a Jehovah's Witness, we also discussed law, order, and the Apocalypse. We agreed it was nigh, although for different reasons. He even tried to convert me before I left, but I reassured him that Jesus and I were on a first-name basis, much like me and G.B. So he didn't try to arrest me, but as I was walking across the lobby to exit, relieved to have gotten off scot-free, he called out, "Miss?"

I turn around and he goes, " 'Behold a pale horse: and his name that sat on him was Death.' " I gave him the thumbs-up sign and kept going. I was halfway through the revolving door when he yelled after me, " 'The name of the star is called Wormwood!' "

I had a parking ticket on my windshield, but that was it. For once I had been lucky. Though not as lucky as G.B., who wasn't even subject to interrogation in the first place. That's the bottom line with insanity: if you don't have a large stage to play on, it can be kind of a letdown. Because people have reflexes, they'll tend to lock up a gal like me if she comes at them swinging an ax with a manic gleam in her eye. Whereas a guy like G.B. is just too far away for them to see. And tends to send, for example, a surface-to-air missile to do his dirty work for him. That's why the well-heeled lunatics among us head straight for the halls of government and large industry to ply their trades. It's the only place they're free to express their personality. The rest of us have to either walk the straight and narrow or settle for the gutters, the asylums, or disability.

And it's not enough to be independently wealthy, with a check coming in from Sotheby's. You have to have a foothold in the community. That was the conclusion that I came to when I noticed, the night after my interrogation, that an unmarked car was following me.

I saw it parked under the dead weeping willow two houses down, with a guy in the front seat. It was still there in the morning; it followed me to the grocery store and back and the issue was settled. I could only assume the sheriff was less clueless than his deputy, but it was still a flagrant waste of taxpayers' money. I lodged a complaint after two days of surveillance, but I had to get a lawyer to wave harasssment papers in the air for me before the county would leave me alone.

And then the war was over. By the time the Kurds rose up a couple of weeks later, per G.B.'s advice, we were high-tailing it outta the Gulf. Here today, gone tomorrow, was our philosophy. Like I said before, no long-term plan was put in place. No, we had to get out of there pronto or it would be another Vietnam, in the words of G.B. Of course, once we were gone, S.H.'s Republican Guardsmen stamped the rebels down mercilessly.

The day of the cease-fire I celebrated jubilantly. No more Baby Duck for me: I bought a bottle of Dom Pérignon and a half pound of beluga caviar. In a candlelit ambience with the TV, I toasted G.B. late into the night for his short, glorious war and its streamlined impunity. I sang two verses of "John Brown's Body" and danced with my reconstructed effigy, having ceremoniously removed all the rusting nails from its Styrofoam-peanut-stuffed body. Finally, I have to admit, I lay with it in my bed, though not in the biblical sense. The effigy and I entered the dreamless sleep of the guilty side by side on our backs, legs splayed on the futon; and there was something delicious about our companion-ship that night, something as warm as cradling a doll in my arms when I was a little kid.

We'd done it again: history. "Again" for the world, that is, but a first for G.B. and me.

3. Thyroid Scare

On the surface, selling arms to a country that sponsors terrorism, of course, clearly, you'd have to argue it's wrong, but it's the exception sometimes that proves the rule.
—VICE PRESIDENT GEORGE BUSH, August 1987

Hey, I've got to go fishing. It's much more important than doing this.
—PRESIDENT GEORGE BUSH, July 12, 1991, during questioning by reporters on Iran-Contra allegations

As G.B. remarked, shortly after I moved to DC, to a group of student hecklers who were shouting "Bush lies" while he was giving a public address at their university, "We must conquer the temptation to assign bad motives to people who disagree with us."

So true. For everywhere around us lie Purity and Goodness, as G.B. knew so well.

In the beginning I had a difficult time adjusting to my new home in the Capital. A bare few city blocks from the majestic Casa Blanca the neighborhoods looked like skid row. Transients frolicked in the fields of concrete with rusty blades, syringes, and broken-necked forty-ounce bottles. And worse still, the day after the speech, on May 5, terror struck the country and me. The unthinkable occurred when 41 went down with an irregular heartbeat. Atrial fibrillation.

Many of my fellow citizens, I believe, were sleepless that night solely because they were selfishly haunted by the specter of Acting President D.Q. Personally, I was sleepless out of pure fear that G.B. might be taken from us and thus removed from the sphere of possibility while things were still unconsummated between him and me. In the spiritual sense, I mean. I became convinced that if I fell asleep, my lack of vigilance would mean the end of G.B., and with him the noble future of the country—be it in fire or ice.

So I took Vivarin and stayed awake all night and through the next day. By then G.B. was back on the job, but he was wired with a portable heart monitor. For three full hours in the afternoon I said prayers to various gods, hedging my bets by including Allah, Vishnu, and Shiva the Destroyer. I even sacrificed several of my favorite items of G.B. memorabilia to the candle flame, figuring that might count as voodoo. Like the minister in my parents' church used to say, prayer is an Equal Opportunity Employer.

Then I consumed seven bags of potato chips to keep up my strength. I held them on my upper chest, as I lay on my back in front of the TV, and scooped piles of them gracefully into my mouth with the aid of gravity. For dessert, I ate four pints of Vermont's finest ice cream. I was nobly abjuring alcohol in order to stay lucid and alert in the event of national catastrophe.

Still, after forty-eight hours of no sleep, my nerves were on edge and I cried during the commercials. Whenever the Stars and Stripes waved over a car dealership or stirring music heralded a breakthrough in hemorrhoid treatment technology, I sobbed raggedly. And when newscasters dropped their casual allusions to G.B.'s life-threatening ailment, I clenched my hands into fists and scraped long peels of skin off my palms with my gnawed fingernails. The raw flesh stung and bled, but I held off on applying hydrogen peroxide or Band-Aids. I was superstitious and believed that if President 41 was suffering, I had to suffer, too. There was a symmetry to my relationship with G.B., a balance that had to be respected.

On May 7 the chief attending Presidential physician, Dr. Burton Lee, announced that the atrial fibrillation had been caused by an overactive thyroid gland. It was treatable and there was no cause for further alarm, he said. I opened my curtains to let in the light of day; I took a walk around the block. I was slightly relieved, but not fully reassured. That night I slept fitfully, waking up at two-hour intervals, wide-eyed and apprehensive. Lapsing once more into a light and tortured sleep, I thought I saw the New World Order collapsing around me. Chaos ruled the streets and the starving masses stole my wide-screen TV. I told them not to eat it, but they defied me.

My unease was vindicated on May 9, when I heard on the news that G.B. had experienced another bout of heart irregularity the night before. Again, we were in synchronicity. He was given a dose of radioactive iodine and cautioned away from his grasping grandchildren due to the radioactivity.

But G.B. was his old self after a couple of weeks, playing his customary speed golf with a vengeance. He even flung a club at one of his Secret Service men, in boyish exuberance. And I recovered, too, albeit slowly. I was not unnerved by his diagnosis with Graves' disease, nor by the speculation in the liberal press via-à-vis the connection between hyperthyroidism and irrational behavior. Pathetic attempts by certain well-known L.B. MDs to publicize the link between Graves' and emotional instability—implying Graves' had affected G.B.'s foreign policy—seemed irrelevant to me. The way I saw it, G.B.'s insanity was God-given, like the birds and the bees. It was part of a grandiose master plan. (For the end of History.)

Still, the shock of his sudden near-death experience had rattled me. I felt it was of paramount urgency that we meet before his reelection campaign got off the ground. For in those days I was convinced G.B. would serve his full eight-year sentence, just like me. And to get close to him, I initially chose to pursue a simple and straightforward strategy: I sent a personal check made out in the amount of $50,000 to the GOP.

Sure enough, I instantly began to receive a slew of embossed invitations to Republican fund-raisers. The third one asked me to attend a gala $1,000-a-plate dinner benefit in Georgetown, at which remarks would be delivered by, among others, B. and G.B. I called in my RSVP, mailed off the check, and then stared at myself in a full-length mirror.

I was giddy, but oddly nervous. I wanted G.B. to be bowled over by me, but not literally. I knew I wasn't your average thin, glamorous cover girl; and though I don't want to be, I understand their appeal to the opposite sex. For an emaciated woman is that much easier to strangle.

But it's difficult to be right when so many others are wrong, so I decided I would try to trim down for my first meeting with G.B. Of course, I wished to remain statuesque; but we all must have goals, and I felt my ideal weight was about 280.

I hired a personal trainer named Elron, who had long blond hair and wore turquoise flip-flops. With his aerobics tutorials, body toning, and Nautilus assistance for two hours a day, along with special "power" shakes he made me in the blender containing something he called blue-green algae, I was soon dropping weight like payloads off a B-52. Within a week, in fact, I was making my mark on the bathroom scale at a mere 286. Elron called his get-fit routine The Personality Army and drafted me as a Private. I wasn't sure about that, but since he had to tell me what to do anyway, I figured it didn't make much of a difference.

Elron recommended a friend of his to furnish the condo for me, and I gave the designer, Randy, Carte Blanche to make my home a "showroom." At least, that was how he put it. And Elron made himself available to me after work hours as well, for more informal fitness sessions that improved my cardiovascular endurance. I rewarded him handsomely with small gifts like watches, cuff links, and once a diamond earring, as well as money.

To prepare for the meeting psychologically, I scripted a number of speeches to make to G.B. I jotted my thoughts on colored index cards whenever inspiration came to me and left the cards all over the house with phrases on them. I practiced conversational gambits in front of the mirror, into a tape recorder, and even into a camcorder. Then I watched the video of myself on TV and tried to work on my facial tics, such as licking my lips repeatedly. Elron and Randy helped a little in terms of designing my wardrobe and a Hair Concept for me.

Finally the big night arrived. I was dressed to the nines for the gala in a long, spangled evening dress and fake-fur stole; I'd had a facial, a manicure, and an herbal wrap, since nothing was too good for G.B. Elron was serving as my escort in white tie and tails and a glittering silver cummerbund. When we arrived at the venue, we were directed to a table right beside the stage; I could hardly believe my luck. But then we sat down and introduced ourselves to our dining companions, and I realized the excellent location of the table was intended to offset the tedium of the assembled company.

To my left was a captain of industry, bald, red in the face, and sporting a golf tie clip; to my right was a face-lifted dowager who seemed to be suffering from an acute neurosis. Throughout the long-winded opening address—during which we were told that G. and B.B. had been held up in traffic on the way from Virginia and would be arriving late, to speak after dessert—the dowager repeatedly blew her pinched nose into a succession of yellow tissues from pocket packages in her purse, which she then piled before her on the table in the approximate shape of a pyramid. These were so unsightly that the wait staff was compelled to remove them regularly, without the benefit of protective gloves. I thought I was going to evacuate involuntarily. Elron was also disgusted. He sauntered off to the cash bar, where he stayed until we were served the after-dinner coffee.

Meanwhile, the captain of industry regaled me with his rags-to-riches story—his mutual-fund empire had been founded on novelty paper clips—and then with graphic anecdotes concerning the drawn-out death of his third wife from an obscure parasite contracted on a luxury cruise to Bali. This gentleman was sorely lacking in perceptivity. Several times I dropped hints that should have given him pause as to my interest in his conversation, remarks such as "I just don't care" and "Shut your trap." But from the cold-soup course to the chicken, he continued to natter on about Indonesian maladies. I even kicked him twice under the table and pinched his arm viciously, to no avail.

He nodded, talked, and chugged liquor as I tried to concentrate on my plan of action, but it was uphill going. Would G. and B.B. stand in a receiving line and shake all of our hands? Would I have to thrust myself between them? For how long could I hold G.B.'s hand without arousing attention, and would he bend his head down to catch my sensual whisper? I'd sent him photographs of me (from the neck up), but that had been almost a year before. I studied my index cards while the dowager rooted in her handbag for nasal spray and the industrialist stabbed at his chicken breast viciously, like it was going to flap its wings and make for higher ground. I couldn't decide which conversational approach to settle on for my encounter with G.B.; there was a chance he wouldn't be shaking hands at all, and in that case I'd have to bolt for the stage at the conclusion of his remarks. Not so easy in the gown I was wearing, plus which the Secret Service might stop me with a couple of hollow-points to the cranial region if I moved too quickly.

You can imagine how ticked off I was when, over the dessert course—a slimy pudding topped with a sprig of plant life—an embarrassed event organizer stepped up to the dais. I couldn't hear what she was saying at first because the industrialist was talking loudly into my left ear. I couldn't understand either of them. "What?" I said. "Pardon, what was that?" I meant, what had the organizer said, but the industrialist stretched his baggy, purple lips wide, the better to enunciate clearly. "Intestinal *worm*," he repeated.

People were getting out of their seats all over the room, crumpling their napkins on the tables and grabbing their coats, talking and looking irritated. I turned to the dowager. "What did she say?" I asked.

"Not coming," she told me. "President can't make it. Traffic, and then emergency."

Apologies were tendered by the spokeswoman, apparently, but they did nothing to console me. There was such a buzz in the room I couldn't hear them anyway. I was pissed as hell. I looked toward the bar but I couldn't see Elron, and I felt myself getting extremely hot under the collar. Even the floral carpeting beneath my feet was starting to look like Sodom and Gomorrah, I was so full of rage. Lilies were fat cherubs perpetrating ugly acts on yellow roses and red tulips. I was staring at the carpet between my feet, seething, when the industrialist slapped his hand down on my thigh and said for the third time, "So I said to him, 'Well, bless me, why *shouldn't* a paper clip be pink or green?' "

I have to admit, I lost my patience. I'd heard the life story once too often, including the moment of epiphany that made his fortune. I slapped my own hand down on top of his and peeled the fingers backward lickety-split, until he shrieked. And then I sliced the side of my hand into his right knee, which had been snuggling up against mine throughout the meal like the snout of a horndog. I'm no karate expert per se, but it had to have hurt. While he was holding up his trembling hand and whining, I got up and made for the coat check, where I found Elron in close conversation with a busboy.

Problem was, the paper-clip magnate had some kind of bodyguard/chauffeur, who turned out to be waiting for me outside the service entrance. Elron's brawn couldn't have counted for less: as soon as the guy went for my stomach with a balled fist, Elron was huddled against the wall, practically covering his face with his hands. But the driver was almost as ancient as his master, and although he put a brave face on it, he was weaker than me. I was just about to have to knee him in the groin when, luckily for him, Mr. Pink Paper Clip finally tottered out the door himself and raised his hand for the poor guy to heel. Turned out he liked the looks of Elron and offered him a ride home. Oddly enough, Elron accepted.

I had spent almost $60,000 on the fruitless venture, all told, only to be foiled by Beltway gridlock. As I drove home alone in my new Town Car, gritting my teeth, I experienced a rare rush of compassion for lobbyists. Morose, I stopped at a 7-Eleven and bought miniature chocolate-covered donuts to assuage my grief. After I ate them, I fired Elron on his answering machine.

His friend Randy's bill for $84,000, including furnishings, arrived the next morning. After paying it grudgingly, I bent my back to new schemes. With the end of the war, G.B. seemed to have forgotten all about S.H.; it no longer bothered him that the former Fuehrer was still walking around bold and free as you please. But his disinterest was no surprise to me. We both had other fish to fry: in his case, a little R&R after the cessation of hostilities; in my case, outreach and communication.

On June 16, while visiting L.A., he dropped a hint he might not run in '92. If, and only if, he was in good health, he said, "I'd owe it to the American people to say, 'Hey, I'm up for the job for four more years.' " This was a red herring, intended to intensify our latent yearning for a second term with G.B., because his health was fine. That very same day, he was so excited about making it to a tennis game that he took off for the courts in a hurry, forgetting to take with him his personal physician and his aide. To say nothing of the ever-present military officer who carries the suitcase containing the secret Presidential codes for launching nukes.

4. Supreme Justice

The fact that he is black and a minority had nothing to do with [the nomination] in the sense that he is the best qualified at this time.

—PRESIDENT GEORGE BUSH
to reporters, July 1, 1991

Clarence Thomas received what was arguably the worst rating ever given to a Supreme Court nominee . . . when the ABA said "qualified," it really meant barely acceptable.

—PHELPS AND WINTERNITZ, *Capitol Games*

While public attention was fixed on the hearings, G.B. craftily wielded his veto again to crush a bill extending unemployment payments to 2 million layabout citizens. Meanwhile there were rumors around town that tainted water at the White House was contributing to the various autoimmune disorders suffered by 41, his wife, and their stupid quadruped Millie. B.B. was floundering along in the losing battle against illiteracy, and I was preparing for the launch of a major two-pronged outreach campaign. I had contracted the services of a professional graphic designer to assist in executing my vision, as well as an expert in pyrotechnics.

I have to explain something. Now, I'll be the first to admit that my early promise in life hasn't yet been fulfilled. Despite being among the best and brightest in my sixth-grade class, where I was twice awarded a Math Excellence certificate in the field of Basic Arithmetic, I've never procured employment that doesn't involve punching a time card. I could blame it on my parents, I guess, but I can't really fault them for preferring reruns of *Gilligan's Island*, *All in the Family*, and later *Miami Vice* to the task of rearing me. From the time I was two or three, I was pretty much left to my own devices; by the time I was seven, even the AFDC checks were coming to me. Mom and Dad just sat in front of the TV, all day and most of the night.

Be that as it may, by late 1991 I was thinking of them vaguely but fondly—almost as if they were different people entirely—and wishing them well wherever they might be. I would have been in touch, only somewhere along the way—I think it was during my third year in Min—I forgot Dad's first name. A psychological block. We had been a traditional family: I always called him Dad, and my mother did, too, at least when I was in the TV room. She would always talk about him in the third person. Like "Dad needs the remote, Rosemary" or "Change the channel back to Dad's game now, Rosie." Come to think of it, the guy was practically a deaf-mute, he talked so rarely. Anyway, the jailhouse shrink said I was erasing his first name from my memory due to the feeling of betrayal I had because no one had stood up for me at the trial, and no one ever came to visit me. I heard my mom and dad had moved, but we have a common last name, and the amount of research required to track them down seemed prohibitive when I was released.

Anyway, my early promise has yet to be kept, so to speak. I remain convinced that it *will* be kept at some future time—on the day when I break out of the fragile, purely temporary eggshell of my current mind-set, physical form, and personality.

But until that day came, in the years following my jail term, I was resolved to avoid my forebears indefinitely. I wanted to have something to show for the passing of time before I saw them again. However, in the midst of my creative campaign consultations, my parents found me. They had employed a detective agency and then sent a spinster aunt, who lived nearby in Maryland, to call on me. She turned up on my doorstep drawn and disheveled, carrying a small, wilting bouquet of white flowers.

"Rosemary?" she quavered when I opened the door in my workout shorts and spandex tank top, fresh from my StairMaster regime. "Jesus Lord, you've got big! You're big as a house, Rosemary."

Instinctively, I slammed the door in her face, shocked by the blast from my past. I soon relented when I heard her moan and slump against it. She was over eighty, a diabetic, and exhausted from her journey. I carried her in and plied her with cold water followed by unsweetened iced tea.

She told me that both my parents were ailing, with high blood pressure and clogged arteries, and residing together in an Assisted Care Home for the Mobile Elderly. She commented several times on the furnishings of my apartment, and on the upscale appearance of the building itself. Then she told me my parents were receiving Inhumane Treatment. Their TV privileges were limited to eight hours a day, and they only got one trip to the mall every week. "Why don't you visit them at least, Rosemary?" she whined plaintively.

I told her I had a rigorous work schedule, and no time for a personal life. "My talents have been recognized at last, and I am very busy. I am a freelance contractor working closely alongside the federal government. President George Herbert Walker Bush, in fact."

"The President! My Lord. Really?" She sipped awkwardly at her iced tea, confused by the lecture since she is none too bright, sitting forward on the couch with her handbag on her knees.

"The President, yes. I share counseling duties with C. Boyden Gray."

"Oh my. I see."

"Boy is a white supremacist. The Thomas nomination was all his idea. Clarence was the only anti-minority black guy they could find. Sadly, he is also a pornography aficionado who drives a black Corvette he purchased with borrowed funds. Not perfect for a Supreme Court justice. And he tends to be a little outspoken in terms of female sexuality. As you may have noticed, it has caused significant problems. I advised against it. But the President had to throw a bone to C. Boyden. It was becoming all too clear that he prefers me."

"Lordy!"

We sat in silence for a moment while I mulled over my most recent fax to the White House, on the subject of C.T., and she glanced around wide-eyed at my many framed snapshots of myself and G.B. Doctored, of course, since the photo ops had not yet materialized, but no doubt impressive to the layperson's eye.

At the end of the interview I sent her packing with a generous check, hoping the funds would serve to keep Mom and Dad happy. At the very least, they would be able to afford their own twenty-seven-inch screen. "Family and faith are the cornerstones," I told her, citing Mr. G. After all, it was small change to me.

Later that day I began marking my calendar with events to be held by the Barbara Bush Foundation for Family Literacy. For the campaign I was planning was half-sales and half-smear. The smear initiative involved, I have to concede, B.B., whose ouster as First Lady I regretfully determined was up to me. To accomplish my aims it would be helpful to besmirch her lily-white reputation and cast her into the mud. So that, faced with her disapprobation by the American public, G.B. would feel no qualms about divorce.

I had not enlisted professional assistance for the smear portion of my offensive, which may have been where I committed my primary error. The smear attempt began auspiciously enough, when I successfully ambushed B.B. at a

Goodwill Book Sale in early October. She was making an appearance for photographers and pretending to read fanciful tales to various children who would have preferred to be watching TV—all of whom were members of visible minorities.

She wore a turquoise apron over a garish royal blue jacket; her trademark gold and pearl earrings; and what I took to be a quadruple string of pearls, at once brassy and ostentatious. No doubt they were paste, since she was completely surrounded by young persons she surely must have regarded as potentially thieving gutter scum.

Masquerading as a volunteer, I drew one kid aside and gave him a hundred-dollar bill, a magazine, and a set of instructions. He nodded eagerly and ran back to the gaggle of urchins, thrusting himself into their midst; then, to my throat-closing thrill of joy, he sidled up to B.B. and pushed the glossy periodical into her hands—I had opened it, for her eyes only, to a craftily inserted double-page spread featuring Winnie the Pooh—and begged innocently, "Read this, lady!"

I squatted in the corner on my haunches, adjusted my zoom lens, and clicked a single historic shot of her smiling at him in her grandmotherly way and raising the magazine for all to see, as she adjusted her reading glasses. The cover featured two naked men kissing.

What must have been her subsequent dismay I did not bother to record for Posterity. I was retreating, camera clutched tightly, through the fire exit, already hoarding my achievement zealously. All the way home I carried the camera delicately yet fiercely, like it was a Fabergé egg. Once safely in the apartment, I removed the film, stared at it in near-disbelief in my own mastery, and then placed it on a shelf when I went to answer the doorbell.

As it happened, the priceless Kodak moment I had recorded will never come to light. Because later that afternoon, while some deliverymen were moving out my leased weight-training equipment, one of them accidentally knocked the film off the shelf with an elbow and then, as I lunged forward with a scream, cracked the canister open with the metal base of my rowing machine.

But I was not going to be beaten so easily. I decided to follow through with the second prong of my attack, despite the fact that B.B.'s reputation remained unsullied. I knew, on some level, that the laws of common sense were against me; but I could not have cared less, frankly. When I felt pangs of doubt and insecurity, I liked to remind myself that I was filthy rich. I told myself I would never have to punch a time clock again. And as long as I had the funds to retain a high-priced lawyer, not even insanity would constitute a liability. In fact, it would only work in my favor, for in this excellent competitive economy acts of megalomania are cost-effective advertising. As zealously as G.B. had pursued his war in the P.G., I was pursuing my domestic campaign to become First Lady.

That was how it came to pass that one blustery autumn dusk, with red and yellow leaves skittering over the concrete, I drank a cup of hot Earl Grey tea with honey, donned a parka, scarf, and woolen hat, and drove the Town Car to a parking lot in downtown DC. There I climbed into the cab of a monstrous eighteen-wheeler whose sides were emblazoned with the phrase *Call Me G.B.* in six-foot-high letters. My graphic designer, who most often worked on magazine ads for 1-900 numbers, had recommended a script that closely resembled tongues of flame, for maximum visibility. I had agreed. Writ large beneath these red, pink, and orange Day-Glo words was my own telephone number; and both sides of the truck were lit from above and below like a Broadway marquee. (I had decided, as you may have discerned, that I had to plan my publicity campaign boldly.)

You may think, privately, that the scheme was outrageous. But, as my consultant ad agency assured me, the more outrageous the better in today's climate of desperate product differentiation. A President is a difficult market to corner, and in lieu of high-saturation advertising we had to go for shock value.

I sat in the passenger seat beside the truck's owner-operator, Mel, who had a harelip and a ragged cough and was none too friendly, and arranged the leaflets in the box on my lap. Mel refused to engage in small talk, but I would not allow his surliness to depress me. In no time at all we were cruising past Union Station, the Capitol, the Mall, and finally the Casa Blanca itself, with a loud, barker's version of my voice repeating the seductive gospel at high volume from a speaker above our heads on the cab roof: "Call me, G.B. George Herbert Walker Bush, call me."

It is surprisingly difficult to orchestrate a White House drive-by and fireworks display. The logistics were a headache, I can tell you. Mel, whom I had located through a helpful Teamsters' local, had been deeply reluctant to deploy his vehicle for advertising purposes in the vicinity of the buildings that housed our head of state and bicameral lawmakers—even for the equivalent of one year's salary, which I paid him without complaining. He feared public-nuisance penalties, and possibly federal charges. I had to sign a waiver and a statement attesting it was all my idea, and then I had to prepay his insurance for the next three years.

As we rolled into position in front of the W.H., I flipped open my new cellular phone to give the go-ahead to my pyrotechnics guy, but it wasn't working. I was picking up only static. Interference, or something. I tapped the earpiece insistently, but the static only tore louder into my eardrum. By the time my pyrotechnician finally started setting off my five minutes of fireworks, my fingers were freezing on my binoculars, which had still not picked up any silhouetted human forms in the White House windows.

I became frustrated quickly. My signage had clearly not

been sighted by G.B., despite the ear-piercing volume of our loudspeakers, because there were few pedestrian spectators and no news vans at all. No one even seemed to be watching my red, white, and blue rockets as they scored the sky with pale streaks, low on the horizon. Their trails resembled wobbly lines of chalk on a dirty blackboard, they were so puny and far away. They were also soundless—hardly the booming, branching umbrellas and candelabra of riotous color I'd anticipated.

The binoculars did not pick out—as I had hoped they might with my razor-sharp eye for the gaunt physique of President 41—G.B. looking on from the family quarters. However, after we'd been parked in our high-profile location for over half an hour, they *did* pick out three sleek, black, official-looking choppers approaching us from the east. And then there was a phalanx of cop cars, surrounding the truck in a semicircle. They barked at us through a bullhorn, ordering us to get out of the vehicle immediately and following up this request with ugly threats about our legal standing. I smiled and waved through the window cheerfully, as if I didn't understand what they wanted; but Mel was less easeful and swore out a stream of invective longer than my arm.

Ultimately, what surprised me was not that he turned on me under stress—we had no real bond, except for my money—but the speed with which he did so. A group of rubberneckers had gathered on a strip of brown, frostbitten grass across from the truck and were gawking; the military helicopters hovered nearby roaring like thunder, then finally swept up and away, leaving us to the infantry. There were a couple of half-muted sirens and then the shock of floodlights; I couldn't see a thing in the blinding glare. I wasn't scared; just pissed and a little disappointed at the lack of press. But Mel was a wuss. He practically leapt out of the cab once he heard the click of gun safeties and saw the snipers kneel down in formation. He raised his hands in the air and stumbled away from me yelling, "The fat lady's fuckin' crazy," at the top of his lungs, before the cops had a chance to draw breath.

I'd heard that before. It didn't bother me.

But given the sheer number of severe-looking law enforcement personnel in the vicinity, his slander was a boon to me. Having the other G.B.-related collar in my disciplinary history would certainly serve as a strike against me if the Feds had any record of the incident—particularly in light of my other ties with the criminal justice system. I opted for Plan B, which involved playing my temporary-insanity role to the hilt. I wish I could say I had been more creative, but I was under severe time constraints and had to improvise in a hurry. Thus, as soon as I stepped out the passenger door, I dropped trou.

Almost before I had begun streaking toward the fence around the Casa Blanca lawn, two meaty law enforcers were on top of me. I don't know why they felt a need to grab me by the upper arms, force me onto my knees, and pin me to the ground, but they did. I'm sure they chalked it up to National Security. About half a minute later someone hurriedly threw a blanket over my exposed bottom half. And one of the uniforms holding me said to the crowd, loudly and pompously, "Nothing to see here."

To make a long story short, it was an outreach effort that failed resoundingly. I was given probation and a fine and kept in a psych ward for a little over ten days. This time the mental-health professionals charged with the task of examining me were more proficient than their counterparts at the sheriff's department; I enjoyed their various testing routines and spent my leisure hours relaxing productively.

I figured the key was to persuade them I was lovesick but not homicidal, so I talked at length about my belief that the benevolent spirit of G.B. had lived in an aloe plant I had. And I cultivated hobbies that I hoped might interest them clinically. These included making collages and fashioning primitive busts of G.B. out of Play-Doh. Also, I pulled Harlequin and Silhouette romances off the shelf in the patient lounge and glued G.B.'s head over the other men's faces on the covers; then I glued my own right on top of the women's. During protracted sessions with a psychologist who specialized in obsessive-compulsive disorders, I went through the books with Liquid Paper and a pen and inked in our names where those of the main characters used to be. "George Bush gathered Rosemary to him, the burnished skin on his strong arms bronze in the candlelight. 'I love you,' he murmured breathlessly. 'I'm so sorry. I never meant to hurt you, my sweet red-blooded mystery.' "

But G.B. doesn't talk like that, as I told the shrink, smiling vaguely as I reviewed my handiwork with her looking over my shoulder. He doesn't like to say sorry. As he put it, "I will never apologize for the United States of America, ever. I don't care what the facts are." Standing tall, G.B. So I rewrote various passages for the purpose of realism and showed the passages proudly to Dr. Dee. "George Bush gathered Rosemary to him, the pale skin on his spindly arms silver in the candlelight. 'We will work hand in hand,' he announced quite warily. 'When America says something, America means it.' "

She nodded and gazed sadly at me.

I was released on an outpatient basis right before the basting and browning of turkeys, with nothing to show for the escapade save an ankle bracelet for the purpose of electronic monitoring by the FBI. And I had completed an informal, ad hoc study of the mental-health industry, which had served to confirm my original hypothesis on the subject. Clearly, the unholy trinity of psychiatry, psychology, and psychotherapy is little more than an effective psy-ops tool wielded by the L.B. By persuading the P.B. and the G.P. that our problems all stem from ourselves, the L.B. hopes to distract us from the fact that they are quietly leeching all the blood out of the body of society.

They are deathly afraid of the all-American grit and determination of self-educated women like me.

Still, I had to admit that a number of my strategies had misfired. It was time to turn over a new leaf.

5. Out, Damned Commies!

I will say frankly that I have mixed feelings today.
—MIKHAIL GORBACHEV to
President George Bush, in a letter discussing
Gorbachev's resignation, December 25, 1991

The horseshoe pit where you threw that ringer is still in
good shape!
—PRESIDENT GEORGE BUSH to
Mikhail Gorbachev, discussing by telephone
Gorbachev's resignation, December 25, 1991

Soon after G.B. had canceled his trip to Asia to stay home and concentrate on the recession, I began to participate in public tours of the White House. I went as often as I could, often joining three successive tours in one day by purchasing scalped tickets. I wanted to avoid arousing suspicion in the wake of the truck incident, so I chose to sport a variety of disguises. I bought six expensive wigs in different styles and colors; putty for the sculpting of false noses; a slew of cosmetics and costumes; and several highly costly custom-made props to distract from the undeniable innate consistency of my dynamic social presence. These included a walker, a wheelchair, a cane, a leg brace, a hearing aid, platform shoes, colored contact lenses, a colostomy bag, and a portable IV. I calculated, quite correctly as it turned out, that these accessories of the infirm and elderly would signal to the tour guides that they should treat me respectfully.

I suspected that, if I persisted in placing myself in the vicinity of G.B. day after day, sooner or later the Hand of Destiny would lean down to nudge us. So I checked in on his travel schedule and appointments every morning in the *Washington Post* and other news sources and made sure I did not enlist myself on tours when he was absent from the city on diplomatic businesss or had a public speaking engagement locally. In purely statistical terms, I was well aware that I was betting on a long shot, but risk is the true currency on which fortunes are based.

Perhaps unfortunately, I was dressed as a trailer-park hooker when the moment arrived. It was only my thirty-second tour. The geriatric getup had become a risk suddenly, for I had had the same tour guide twice in a row the previous day. This was an extraordinary coincidence, since over four thousand persons visit the White House on an average day. Still, on the afternoon tour I thought I caught her gazing at me in vague recognition. On the morning tour I had been confined to a wheelchair and claimed paraplegia when she engaged me briefly in conversation; on the afternoon tour I had changed because my back was aching and was using the walker and wearing the colostomy bag in plain view. I also purported to be deaf, so that she could not hear my voice a second time; but nonetheless I believe that in the Red Room, beside a simpering portrait of Dolley Madison, she was staring at me.

I did not wish the ever-present Secret Service man to be alerted by her curiosity. So I had temporarily traded in the complex trappings of senescence for a leather miniskirt, black fishnet nylons with a visible garter belt, stiletto heels, and a zebra-striped midriff bustier, all augmented with a teased red wig and long purple fake fingernails. I chewed and popped bubble gum audibly and spoke in what I hoped was a Texan twang.

It was a deep, deep cover.

I caught sight of him in the flick of an instant, at the

end of the hall, as my tour group was milling around at the door of the Diplomatic Reception Room. I was feeling dizzy from the wraparound panoramic wallpaper. Sorry for the cliché, but it was like time had stopped. He was walking fast, with four men in gray suits bobbing and weaving on his flanks. Wobbling on my high heels, I felt disoriented. I clutched at the doorframe, swallowed my gum, and almost choked. Tides welled up in me, speeding up my heartbeat and causing me to break out in a cold sweat even though sheets of heat were rising in my temples and pulsing behind my eyes.

He was casually dressed, jacketless with his shirtsleeves rolled up. He had loosened his dark tie. He held a compact phone to his ear. Two of the suits were wearing holsters and headsets; one of them carried a briefcase.

I have to admit that, despite all that had already passed between us, I was momentarily stricken by G.B.'s presence. I mean, just because you're a Catholic doesn't mean you expect to see the weeping Virgin in the flesh. I didn't have time to wonder what chain of circumstance had led him from the family quarters into the public domain; I couldn't stop to consider the effect of the halter top I was wearing as a key component of my whorish disguise. (It permitted open display of a wide swath of bare flesh around my stomach, pocked by the light as leaves are dappled by the summer sun in a tree.) I lost all comprehension of the present minute: my future and G.B.'s history were a shimmering dance of glory.

Interspersed with images of his Inaugural, of him speaking bitingly of Saddam in front of a desert backdrop, saluting the flag and talking fondly of the pet dog Millie, and saying, in 1988, "A kitchen in every pot, I mean a pot in every—!" were visions of us together. I saw us standing on the West Front terrace, a staff topped by an imperious Bald Eagle in my hand, from which the laser beam of Freedom, Democracy, and the Almighty Dollar shone forth. We were the Wild West bandits that controlled the world, whipping six-shooters from our hips and bringing our billions of enemies to their knees. I saw myself wrapped in a flowing stone gown, tall, vast, and kick-ass: the Statue of Liberty.

And as I looked upon myself, my torch held high to flame against the starred and striped unending sky, I understood for the first time what G.B. was to me. Noble, yes; a natural statesman and a leader, yes; blue-blooded, yes, with all the history and lineage of Greenwich, CT; but if the truth be told, once the blinders were off the watching world, just an Executive Assistant to me.

And yes, I was carried away on the wave of the Vision; and yes, I leapt with outstretched arms from the crowd of gawking tourists surrounding me, abruptly breaking a heel, twisting my ankle, stumbling, and becoming airborne; and yes, as I flew out aloft over the carpet toward him, I cried, "My soldier! My President! G.B.!"

Yes, that is what occurred, and I will not deny it. I scraped my chin on the carpet and bled copiously, though at the time I scarcely noticed. My teased red wig fell off and lay beside me limply.

Later, I was to write no fewer than three (3) letters to the shoe manufacturer's customer-service department, which I sent along with photographs of my swollen ankle, a sales receipt indicating the newness of the item at the time of its surrender to gravity, and the broken heel. And yet later still, customer-relations representatives were to respond with grotesque impudence that shoes in that particular style were not designed to bear the weight of "full-figured" women like me. They were to offer me, quite condescendingly, a ten-dollar coupon toward a second purchase of their inferior, Third World sweatshop merchandise, and to advise me to invest, this time, in a "flat" or "wedge" style rather than a pump. Following that, I was to threaten litigation, since there had been no warning on the shoe label as to the product's maximum carrying capacity.

But as I was catapulted into the air over the Casa Blanca

carpet, as I landed hard on the floor and somewhere in the near distance there was the tinkle of priceless china shattering, that was all in the future. Shocked by my contact with a hard surface, thick mascara drooling into my eyes with tears of impact, I raised my head. Flat on my stomach with my legs splayed, I reached for my purse. Its contents, including Feminine Hygiene supplies and diet pills in brightly marked red and yellow boxes, were scattered in a wide fan.

And then I noticed, not five feet from me as the crow flies, the concerned face of G.

Unfortunately, at the second that I saw his face, I glanced down and saw that my left breast had broken free of the halter top and was lolling forward on the carpet like a frightened bulldog creeping out of its lair.

I looked up again and our eyes locked momentarily, the blue and the gray. Then G.B. blinked and said quickly, "You—uh, you okay?" He was stuttering slightly; he winced and turned his face away. But as I opened my mouth to answer him, a brave yet teary smile at the ready, a flick of pain shot through my foot and caused me to squeal like a stuck pig. The shriek broke the awkward silence that had settled after my last cry of "G.B.!" had faded. G.B. was immediately backgrounded by one of his Secret Service personnel, who stepped between us and offered me an arm to cling to. In the process, another of his fellow Treasury Department coworkers began to steer G.B. away.

Then the Secret Service officer who was helping me up nodded at the tour guide, spoke into his headset under his breath, and turned, and G.B. glanced back over his shoulder to look at me as I heaved myself off the floor. His quick, lopsided grin clinched everything.

Because first he grinned; then he hid his face behind a raised hand and whispered to one of his companions while he lifted the other hand to wave to the tour group that was cowering behind me. And then his eyes seemed to rest on me briefly again, and a new grin split his face. He laughed. The next second, everyone was laughing. You could say the walls trembled with laughter. To my right, a thin man with sideburns hooted with hilarity until he doubled over and had to dab at his streaming eyes with a hanky; to my left, a teenage girl cackled like a hen until she ran out of breath and started snorting.

A moment later G.B. had stepped through a door and disappeared. I stared after him, barely distracted by the tourists and the bespectacled tour guide hovering around me. Their laughter wound down finally, and then they acted confused and a little embarrassed. One old man helped pick my loose change off the floor, while the stoop-shouldered tour guide proffered a stray tampon furtively.

Some of the more conservatively dressed, anal-retentive women in the group were still tittering. Obviously they thought my humiliation was payback for my streetwalker's attire and brazen femininity. I sneered at one of them as I picked the wig off the rug and stuffed it into my purse. "There are wheels within wheels, you silly twat," I said, and she gasped, shrank back, and fingered her crucifix necklace nervously. After that I was offered no further assistance, and the tour reached its conclusion rapidly. I ambled along at the rear of the crowd with bovine submissiveness, replaying the incident in my mind dreamily until we were out on the street again. Then, in shock, I wandered for over an hour in a downtown parking structure, unable to locate my Town Car.

Later that night, as I mulled over the incident with a tumbler in hand in front of the TV, all I could remember sharply was my Chief Executive retreating hastily down the hall, glancing sidelong at his cohorts and smiling behind his hand. And it became unavoidably clearer to me that 41 had been laughing at, not with, Yours Truly. And a strange new bitterness preyed upon me.

Circa this time the vast, lumbering Soviet empire collapsed to its knees, with the manful assistance of G.B.

1992

1. Capital Gains

Communism died this year. Even as President, with the most fascinating possible vantage point, there were times when I was so busy helping to manage progress and lead change that I didn't always show the joy that was in my heart . . . by the grace of God, America won the Cold War.

—PRESIDENT GEORGE BUSH,
State of the Union address, January 1992

In May 1992, Gorbachev flew to California . . . aboard the gleaming black Forbes Magazine jet, *Capitalist Tool.*
—BESCHLOSS AND TALBOT, *At the Highest Levels*

G.B. had rid the world of the scourge of Communism, if you overlook a billion tenacious Chinese. The way I saw it, that meant I could keep my TV.

Yet on the personal level, it was like he'd defected to the USSR and become a hard-line Stalinist overnight. That was what his smirk had done to me. For weeks I couldn't get the sour taste of it out of my mouth; the memory insinuated itself into my daydreams and made it impossible for me to muster my usual ardor. I tried to adjust my recollection of the White House incident creatively—reframing his facial expressions and body language in a light that was more complimentary to me—but it resisted stubbornly.

When he vetoed a bill that would have given a tax credit for health insurance to poor families, on the grounds that it contained a new tax for the extremely wealthy, I felt a touch ambivalent. In the days of the P.G.W., and my vibrant and proud insanity, I would have been pleased. After all, it's hardly the poor and sick who finance reelection campaigns. But instead I found myself receiving the news nonchalantly. It was like G.B was fading to an even dimmer shade of gray, like he'd shrunk and become puny. His 40 percent approval rating was beginning to seem almost fair.

I lapsed into a sluggish indifference from which not even repeated screenings of the "Read my lips" pledge could rouse me. Vintage footage of G.B. issuing threats to Saddam cheered me up slightly, but only in the way a lonely mother might be solaced (through her tears, bittersweetly) by old home movies of her handsome young son throwing a Frisbee and smiling as he ran backward to catch it on a green lawn on a sunny day.

If that son was dead, hit by a passing truck just as the Frisbee fell.

I was paralyzed. I spent several weeks after my ill-fated visit to the Casa Blanca reclining on my bed in soiled laundry, staring vacantly at the screen and consuming over forty large bags of Cheez Doodles—pretty much in despair. The sun had disappeared, leaving the horizon blank; it was as though the earth had slipped loose from its orbit. At the same time gravity was a dead weight, lying atop me like an old, boozy sailor.

I had been robbed; I had lost everything.

The dreams, the plans I'd harbored for me and G.B., came back at night when I was trying to fall asleep, held back from slumber only by thoughts of lonely death. My former hopes flared out over the dark sky of my past like so many defective missiles from Afghanistan plunging to earth. Exploding silently in the empty landscape.

I barely read the newspapers anymore; I was loath to engage with the world around me. It had proven too disappointing. TV was bad enough; the Texas leprechaun R.P. kept popping up on every other channel wearing a throttleme grin, threatening to oust G.B. by splitting the Nasal-Voiced/Senseless vote.

The hardest part of my disillusionment was not, as you might expect, G.B.'s rudeness to me. His seeming contempt for my person, as I squirmed before him on the floor like a gigantic maggot, might after all have been feigned; or it might have been a trick of the light. It was not a fact, a biblical law, or a concrete reality, but merely a suggestion.

No, what tortured me was *my* contempt for *him*. I could not bear the intimation that G.B. was not what I had held him to be. I was chilled by the fear that what we were dealing with, at base, was nothing more than a petty, common mediocrity. Nothing more, nothing less: just a footnote to the twentieth century.

As you may well agree, even the hint of this dread possibility reflected poorly on me.

And so the greasy bags that had once held Cheez Doodles piled up on both sides of my bed, tipping sideways and upside down and trailing their bright cargoes of orange dust on the floor.

I was hibernating. But every bear must wake up, eventually.

With the first flush of early summer I gleaned from the news that President 41 had a trip to Panama coming up on his sixty-eighth birthday, then a flight down to Rio, Brazil, for the Earth Summit, where treehuggers were congregating en masse, ready to screech out their poignant yet irritating warnings. One morning I stepped into my foyer and saw that a promotional copy of that fine, full-color publication *USA Today* had been dropped through the mailslot for me. I shrugged and picked it up. I wasn't going to go looking for the world, but I was willing to stare at it dully if it offered itself up to me.

And that was when I was lifted out of the Slough of Despond I'd been languishing in. It was a simple trigger, a minor phrase that solaced me in my erstwhile doubts about

G.B. in re his chances of leaving behind a lasting legacy. It was a single sentence on the front page.

> Bush also made it clear he will not sign a treaty on biodiversity, intended to prevent the extinction of animal and plant life around the world.

I'm not afraid to tell you: my relief was like ecstasy.

2. Vomitus

Mr. Bush read aloud from "Harry, the Dirty Dog," to two dozen first graders in the Diplomatic Reception Room of the White House. He told them how his dog, Ranger, had killed a rat.

— *The New York Times,* April 9, 1992

I'm the one son of a bitch around here who thinks I can win.

—PRESIDENT GEORGE BUSH to his aides
on the election campaign, 1992

In late summer of that final year, I began to sense that G.B.'s reelection campaign was faltering. I do not put it too strongly, I think, when I say that his candidacy was acquiring the stink of death.

This impression was confirmed for me when, shortly after G.B. had met with the Russian dipsomaniac Yeltsin to put his John Hancock on a nice-looking nuclear treaty, he vomited on TV. On the occasion of G.B.'s dinner in Asia I entered my living room with three grocery bags just in time to witness his furtive regurgitation into the lap of a surprised Japanese, followed by insipid and sly remarks by commentators. These struck me as disrespectful and ignorant, although I, too, was mildly surprised at the evidence that G.B. possessed a gag reflex.

But when I finally sat down grumbling to watch the rest of the broadcast, I had to smile to myself, knowingly. For it was typical of G.B. that he hadn't elected to vomit on, for

example, the French people or the Swiss. Many of my compatriots wisely resent the Japanese for their discipline and
industriousness and might have felt their hearts gladden at
this televised sign that G.B. shared their distaste. To the last,
G.B. was choosing his foreign targets cunningly.

Then Fate intervened. In a 7-Eleven parking lot, I ran
into someone I knew.

Bessie G.

I first caught sight of her as I emerged from the store
with a couple of family-sized bags of Doodles. She was sitting against the 7-Eleven's finger-smeared glass front on the
dirty concrete, dressed in filthy rags with a Toronto Blue
Jays baseball cap perched backward on her head; she was
slurping from a Hawaiian Punch fruit drink and petting an
ugly pug dog that was seated panting between her legs. I
recognized her by the black roses she had tattooed on her
cheeks, which looked like rotten boils. And I tried to duck
away behind a telephone pole, but it was too late. She'd
already seen me. Her arm snaked out like greased lightning; she grabbed my leg and said the dog was hungry.

He didn't look hungry to me; he looked like a fat wad-
dler. But I was in a hurry to get away, so I dug around in my
coat pocket and handed her a bill. But it wasn't enough.
She wanted to come home with me, being, as it were, of No
Fixed Abode currently.

Now, it may not have been exactly clinical, but Bessie
definitely had multiple personalities. There was a karate
expert named Jojo, who was also a pyromaniac, a blushing
bride from Korea who talked in pidgin and stabbed people
in the left eye with what she called her "chopstick," and a
lecherous German mountaineer. The most powerful one of
all, at least in the joint, was known to the rest of us as Cut-
throat Al and worked in a slaughterhouse disemboweling
old pigs.

So I let her come home with me. And I didn't say a
word when she headed for the kitchen and began to bang

drawers open and shut, apparently looking for liquor. About an hour later my cabinets were cleaned out of everything from Mylanta to V-8, and Bessie G. was snoring loudly with her dog, whose name was General Beauregard, sleeping draped over her feet. Problem was, the next morning I had to go in for a scheduled appointment with the FBI. I left Bessie asleep on my floor, after making sure the wall safe was securely locked. The Feds were removing my ankle bracelet, at long last, and I was looking forward to getting rid of the thing. It had rubbed sores, chafing until the flesh was raw and pulpy.

Returning to the apartment, I wasn't quite as euphoric as I would have liked to be, as I had learned that the lawyer I'd hired to gouge Big Brother for pain and suffering was proving sluggish. Still, I was pleased to be wearing regular socks again and was singing a merry tune as I left the Bureau behind. But when I stepped through my front door and smelled burning, I sensed that all was not as it should be.

Bessie had made a massive pile out of my stuff in the middle of the living room floor and lit it up like a funeral pyre. The peak and one side of the pile was blazing, and my carpet was already scorched black in a ring. I ran back and forth from the kitchen and threw water on the bonfire till the billowing smoke made me cry, then started sorting through my burnt things. First a toilet brush, then a twist of XXL control-top nylons, then a discarded crutch with floral armpit padding and a disposable cupcake baking tray flecked with crusts of frosting. Then my deluxe new food processor split open on the sharp corner of the coffee table. And I started to get pissed.

But that wasn't the worst of it. At the very bottom of the pile I found all my G.B. paraphernalia, including the photos of him and me.

And crushed beneath it all, limbs angled oddly, face torn off his head, was G.B.'s effigy. Slumped and smoldering.

I went into shock. I gritted my teeth in hideous fury, grabbed a curling iron from the pile, and went looking for her. I found her sitting on the can, calmly reading a magazine, and launched a preemptive strike via a kick to the knee. She gave a guttural, choking scream, rose like a jack-in-the-box, and clocked me upside the head, making my left ear ring. Then she tripped me, and we grappled on the floor until I had several scratches on my face and she was yowling and staring at where I'd tagged her with the curling iron, on a bloody ear.

When we were finished, Bessie G. got up off her haunches, face contorted into a cruel grimace as usual, and dragged her carcass out of the apartment. And I sank to the still-melting, still-curling expanse of carpet with my caftan settling in a wide pool around my legs. The odor of burn was strong; a headache set in, so I lugged myself out into the fresh air and collapsed anew onto my cement-floored balcony, where I remained, unmoving, for several hours, in what I now believe to have been a near-catatonic state. I must have closely resembled the Buddha beneath his Tree.

A sequence of visions came to me.

In the gray pool of the sky I saw José the patriot deportee, reading his favorite picture book, *Curious George,* and laughing gleefully at the monkey's antics; José in Russell's kitchen, marveling at the miracle of Jell-O. I saw Lee Ann on break the day before her DUI husband died, smoking a menthol and then flipping it onto the ground and grinding the butt into the sand as she quoted from Scripture and vowed for the third time that week to leave him. He'd just lost the last of their savings on a dog race. I saw Lee Ann getting a back rub from Esperanza, the Senior Quality Assurance Officer, as she read her horoscope out loud to me. "Virgo: surprise new romance in the offing this month. Trust yourself." She'd taken that one as an invitation to fornication and picked up a schizophrenic exterminator that very night at Skullduggery. He gave us a lecture on the different kinds of cockroaches—"You got your German, your Brown-banded, your Oriental, and the biggest ass sucker of 'em all, the American"—and then later, in the parking lot, dislocated her shoulder when she refused to perform certain acts. He drove away in his van with a giant weevil on top and crashed into a tree.

I thought of an embezzler who had bunked with me in Min, hawking prescription pills at a markup in the kitchen for what she called her "college fund" and then crying into her pillow. She cried all the time—keeping us up at night with her endless caterwauling until two strong-willed girls from the inner city stuffed a wad of dirty underwear in her mouth—and finally tried to do herself in with a sharpened spatula. She was removed after that and replaced for a short time by a pedophile from Nevada who was obsessed with card tricks.

Russell, too, dragged himself across the floor of my memory and latched on to my ankle with his toothless gums. And there I was myself, in the forested backlot at grade school, putting my fingers to my lips and daring a skinny Pakistani boy to pull his pants down beside the toolshed and show me his thing. He was so frightened that he peed. There I was jabbing Aunt Rachel's butt with my car keys at Shelly's funeral, repeatedly, and then pretending not to have noticed it when she turned around. (I had been discouraged from attending, but showed up anyway dead drunk. After the service I threw a tantrum, weeping, and smashed the headlights on Rachel's car with a crowbar.)

I saw all these things as I sat bleeding from the nose and mouth on the balcony. And I thought to myself, "Life is a many-splendored thing."

When I finally wandered inside, I noticed that General Beauregard had eaten a watermelon rind and half a pizza box. Subsequently he had taken ill and, when I entered the kitchen, was lying on his back on the floor, emitting low-pitched moans, squat legs pedaling slowly. He was bloated dramatically. Later I would have to take him to the vet to have his stomach pumped.

But at that moment, I could not have cared less. I wandered past Beauregard in a daze, and on through the apartment.

That was when I found out that Bessie G., before she left, had broken open the wall safe and taken all my money. And left me with nothing, except for the dog.

I looked at the deep red designer drapes that Elron's decorator friend had chosen for me; I looked at the full-size stuffed llama and the zebra-skin upholstery, which he had assured me were all the rage. The llama had a rude expression on its face; I slapped it and it fell over with a loud crash. I sat down on the couch, ran my palms over the zebra. I stared at the Tiffany lamps, the velvet chairs with lions' paws, the trophy elk and moose heads Randy had purchased for me; I stared at the wall-size tank of tropical fish; I gazed curiously at the china Kama Sutra figurines that lined the shelves of the inlaid, ebony tallboy he had found in Miami. And I realized that through it all—the insanity, the felony, even the rampant gluttony—I had made only one real mistake.

I had forgotten my brethren, the G.P.

If I had not forgotten my brethren, I would not have stood for the showmanship of Elron or Randy. The G.P. can see straight through bullshit to its heart, and when they see it, they pick it out in the sights of their rifles and they shoot it down. I would not have paid a decorator what used to be four years' salary to hang the carcasses of quadrupeds on my walls and buy $5,000 leather armchairs. I would not have drunk a blue-green algae power shake, invested in acupuncture to quit smoking (which failed miserably), or enlisted in Elron's Personality Army. And above all, I would not have given my money away for the sake of instant gratification. I would have gotten it for free.

I had forgotten my people entirely. Somewhere along

the line I had forsaken them, so to speak. And Bessie G. had come to show me that they were angry. For my people are vulnerable to only one thing.

G.B.'s people.

And he had been faithful to them from the start.

"Much good can come from the prudent use of power," as 41 had remarked in his '92 State of the Union. When we should have been running neck and neck, G.B. and I—our flanks glistening with foam, each leading our respective hordes into the bright dawn of manifest destiny, together trampling with iron-shod hooves over S.H., Noriega, and their ilk, together stampeding boldly across the glamorous ground of international piracy—instead I had weakened and diverted my course. I had tried to run in the rear guard, following after G.B. but far behind, on the heels of my sworn enemy the L.B. It was a testament to my unconscious defection that I had felt strangely ambivalent about G.B.'s stouthearted veto of the unemployment-benefits bill, for my people do not approve of handouts, even to our brothers and our sisters. My people think they should get up off their asses, even if their legs are crippled. My people cherish the dream of lots of money and play the lottery. My people are a proud people, proud and free.

And with that I raised myself up off the couch in determination. I strode across the room and was going to hurl a Kama Sutra figurine onto the floor to join the capsized llama, but then I remembered I could probably get a couple of bucks for it.

So I wandered out onto my balcony again with Beauregard waddling behind me, and I looked down at the dry, beige streets of DC spread out below me like concrete spokes from the wheel of Dupont Circle. The boulevards were ugly. I mourned the passing of G.B.: for what was left of him was only a ghost that moved with no body across the flat screen of my TV.

I now have an ulcer, which I believe dates from the

loss and the humiliation of that blank-skied and windless day.

A week later I watched the election returns, clad in the sombre black of mourning for the end of a political dynasty. Easy come, easy go was how it was, for both myself and G.B.

3. Pardon Me

This, the world's greatest nation.
—PRESIDENT GEORGE BUSH,
concession speech, November 3, 1992

This, the greatest nation in human history.
—PRESIDENT-ELECT BILL CLINTON,
victory speech, November 3, 1992

The next three months were devoted to the dissolution of my one-woman empire, paralleling the decline and fall of G.B.'s. He wasn't a self-promoting guy; the way I saw it, he felt he was above all that. In '88 he'd been presold, like so many tract homes alongside a commuter highway, but in '92 he came up against a skilled salesman and his heart just wasn't in the fight.

No, at the end of it all G.B. was a gray scarecrow in a dunce cap, smiling his thin-lipped smile as he lobbed horseshoes at a rusty spike in the deserted courtyard of a fortress that had once been immense. Ragged kids threw rocks at his stick legs and laughed mockingly, but he thought they were only joking and tried to join in. Hopped around flicking pebbles at his own knees to be a sport and feebly tittering, "Hee, hee, hee."

I harbored a certain nostalgia for what we had had—a steady indulgence of our past relationship, as buoyant as the sea—but it was the kind of resigned yet tender loss you might feel for an incontinent pet with a tumor.

I wasn't flat broke, but when I bunkered down with my checkbook on the table, broke out the last of my hoard of Sapphire gin, and assessed the situation coolly, it soon became plain that I had to sell off my belongings and get a job again. It was back to the drawing board for me.

While I was flogging secondhand espresso makers and furs and packing boxes in preparation for removing myself from DC, and G.B. was doing likewise in the Casa Blanca, a lone eighteen-wheeler was making its way east along Interstate 40. Its bearded driver had just had a conversation with two elderly sisters, whose names were Lynn and Margery. I can see him clearly: hunched over the steering wheel in concentration, he kept his beady eyes fixed on the speedometer, whose needle consistently hovered around 93. He was probably holding the wheel so tightly that his callused, tobacco-stained fingers were white at the knuckles, and he hardly ever raised his CB for the exchange of pleasantries. He was intent on one thing: retribution. He wanted to punish me.

It was, as you might have guessed, Apache.

And in the dead of night soon after Thanksgiving, I was sleeping alongside General Beauregard on my water bed—for which I hadn't received any offers as yet—when my dreams were invaded by an unpleasant sensation. It crept in around the edges. At first it was as if I'd wet myself. In a long, weird dream centered around the dark, graceful mass of a marine mammal (which resembled both a whale and a seal, although within the dream I knew it somehow to be a manatee), I became embarrassed. In the dream, while I was swimming placidly underwater beside the manatee and discussing with her the issue of flag-burning, I discovered I was wearing a diaper. Waterlogged, the diaper unfurled from my waist, floated away behind me, and was lost in the bluc caverns of the sea. The manatee disapproved of this and shunted me away with her slick, leathery hip. I sank and flailed, grabbed on to a stationary blowfish for mooring, and was pricked. Next I grunted and came awake. General Beauregard was no longer in the bed.

As it turned out, Apache had sliced the mattress open with a bowie knife and was sitting beside my bed waiting while the water leaked out over the floor. He was leaning over the slowly collapsing heap with the point of his curved blade held tickling my throat.

"You're gonna get it, fat lady," he said.

I don't know if he would actually have hurt me. Because luckily, the small slit in the bed ruptured suddenly and dramatically at that moment. As water poured forth in a tidal rush beneath me, I dropped away from the knife onto the emptying shell of the mattress. Instincts swift as the speed of light, I rolled away and Apache lost his balance and fell over me. My legs and feet were wet and had no traction; I kicked at him kind of uselessly and pulled his tangled hair. It took me back. And somehow, without thinking, I grabbed for the knife; felt the handle in my palm miraculously; and struck out. Its blade slid into the flesh of Apache's upper arm (but did not touch the bone, I later found out). However, it stuck there, temporarily crippling him.

Shocked at the turn of events, I shrieked and stumbled up, afraid of what he was going to do to me. In a flurry of panic, nightgown, and twisted sheets, I ran screaming from the room, slammed the door behind me, and sat down hard against it, sinking to the floor, trapping Apache just as he threw his weight against it on the inside.

General Beauregard padded up from where he had been cowering beneath a table and licked at my bare toes until, still regaining my breath, I cuffed him and he slunk away. After a few minutes of calm, I ripped a strip off the hem of my flannel nightgown—somewhat painstakingly, since at the same time I had to concentrate on pressing my weight solidly against the panel of the door to counteract the blows raining down from the fists and shoulders of Apache—and shoved it under the door. Apache eventually stopped his pummeling, no doubt to tend to his wound.

As the night wore on, we waged a battle of wills, each trying to deploy psy-ops to suss the other out. Every so often the door would shake with a single assault, when he deemed me absent from my post—wrongly—and then all would grow quiet again. I mulled the situation over in my head, thought back to the time in the basement, and felt more and more righteous that I had stabbed him. Though it had been unpremeditated, I wasn't sorry. It served him right, frankly.

But when dawn came, the novelty of Aggravated Assault had worn off and I was nodding off against the jamb. My portable phone was on an end table about ten feet away, and I knew that I wouldn't be able to dial before Apache would be out the door and in my face with some weapon or other. He kept knives and guns all over his body, as I had seen him proudly demonstrate to Russki. Knives in the boots, gun in the back of his waistband except when he was driving, knife up his sleeve, gun slung under his shoulder like a cop's, he was a walking trigger. I still had my own handgun, stashed in a drawer, but I didn't want to get into a close-range shoot-out with a soldier-for-hire. I had gone head to head with him once before and still regretted it sorely.

I was also regretting that I had not taken the time to train Beauregard properly. Once or twice I pointed to the phone and whispered fiercely, "Fetch!" but he ignored me, merely rumbling in his sleep.

Finally I thought of G.B., and of diplomacy. So, through the door, I asked Apache, "Have we exhausted all peaceful means?" There was no answer. But a diplomat must be patient. "Listen, Apache," I said. "I know you're pissed at me. And I'm sorry I pretended Chrissy was sick. That was low. There's no excuse. But, Apache, not to be crude or anything, but you kind of raped me. I never went to the cops, Apache, after that incident. Out of respect for you and your service to the country, and knowing how life drives men crazy. But I had to get you out of my hair. It was self-defense, Apache."

It was 10 A.M. by the clock on the mantelpiece when he spoke back to me:

"Lemme out. I'm bleeding here."

"I can't fight you."

"Uh-huh."

"I can sit here until all the blood drains from your body, though."

"Just lemme outta here. What are you gonna do?"

This wasn't an artful, sophisticated maneuver, but in my exhausted state it convinced me. I had become indifferent about consequences. Slowly but surely I dragged myself away from the threshold. I picked up the phone and dialed three numbers, 9-1-1, with my shaking left hand, and just as the woman picked up, Apache came out the bedroom door. He'd wrapped the flannel strip around his biceps and was holding it pulled tight with his other hand. It was soaked through with dark blood.

Yet another of our famous détentes. We stared at each other across the room. Raising his bloody arm, Apache rubbed his nose with the back of one hand. He looked pretty pathetic, but appearances can be deceiving. Stalling for time, I gave my name and address to the woman on the other end of the phone. I enunciated clearly. Then I said, "If anything happens to me, there's a guy you should tell the cops about named Apache. From Baton Rouge."

"Is he a threat to you currently?"

"No, I guess not," I said slowly, meeting his eyes. "He's not a threat currently."

While she was lecturing me on 911 protocol, I hung up.

"Oh, fuck it," said Apache.

He slouched over to me and sat down with a thump; I

ambled into the kitchen, opened the fridge, and threw him a can of beer, which he drank while still pulling the bandage taut. As soon as he'd downed the Bud, he leaned back and looked at me out of slitted eyes. "Flesh wound," he said dismissively.

I have to admit it, I thought that was kind of sexy. I mean, the guy's wrist was dripping red stuff like rain off a storm gutter. When I complimented him on his attitude, he didn't say anything, but I could tell he was pleased. After a polite interval I went to the bathroom and brought out my first-aid kit. I cleaned the wound and gave him a new bandage, following his directions. And we got to talking over a pot of gourmet coffee.

I told him about Russell's funeral, and how in the obituary I'd asked the bereaved to send donations to Rolling Thunder. He approved. I asked him why it had taken him so long to come after me. He pulled down his pants and showed me a purple scar, bright as a flower, on his knee. "I was laid up a few months. They hadda put in a fake kneecap," he said. "I had an accident in the truck. Steep downgrade and no braking power."

Over the course of our conversation, which included many fond reminiscences of Russell, I began to notice that Apache was keeping himself quite trim. He had cut the beard into a stylish goatee and was otherwise clean-shaven. The hair on his head was neatly combed. It struck me that he was the only person who knew about my former close rapport with President 41. We were linked by a State secret, after a fashion.

We ate a couple of ham sandwiches and switched from coffee to whiskey and gin. When the sun began to set, we ordered a deep-dish pizza with pepperoni and mushrooms and took our drinks out onto the deck. When it got too cold, we went inside again and Apache built a fire in the fireplace, using a flame-throwing torch he'd brought with him. He also brought in a sleeping bag and we spread it out on the living room floor. And I was astounded by what happened then. Even without the codeine Apache had given me for the persistent ache in my upper arm, I would have forgotten my anguish. One word of warning to my sisters out there in the G.P.: once you've had a mercenary, of your own free will that is, you're ruined for other men.

The next day we lugged the deflated water bed out onto the street and left it huddled on the icy curb for the garbagemen. The water damage to my hardwood floor was extensive. Apache dried the floor out with his flamethrower, but he said that beneath the top layer the wood was still soaked and rotting. And you could still see a large pale stain. I wouldn't be getting my rent deposit back.

While he stayed with me that first week before setting out on a new haul, I learned a lot about his history. He and Russki had retired from their freelance soldiering, it turned out, during the Summer of Love. They hadn't intended to retire; they were just on vacation between the Gaza strip and Cambodia, where they had a gig lined up with a guy named Lon Nol. They decided to take a trip back to the home Republic to relax. Russki wanted to vacation in San Francisco, since he'd never been there before. Apache chose Miami, and they couldn't agree. Finally they asked an Algerian whore to decide the winner. In a contest involving liquor and perseverance, Russell won, Apache admitted ruefully.

"What did she know," I said, and goosed him.

"If I hadda got it up one more time," he mused sentimentally, "I bet you we'd still be living the life today."

For San Francisco had proved to be their downfall. Russell was not a hippie—far from it: he hated them with single-minded zeal and had once emptied the contents of a staple gun into a barefoot flower child strumming on a zither—but he took to psychedelics like a lamb to the slaughter. Meanwhile, Apache had met up with Chrissy's mother, a sophomore at Berkeley. They moved south of the border, onto a compound outside Tijuana, and in 1972 were forced into a shotgun wedding by her insane Cajun father.

With the divorce, two years later, Apache wanted to take up soldiering again, but to get visitation rights he had to be a responsible father. He gave up his dream and went into trucking for the sake of a few long weekends with Chrissy every year.

It was a beautiful story; Apache had lived a tragic life. I found myself weeping. Whether it was from the strength of the nostalgia or the effects of the painkillers I was taking, I can't say for sure. But I was hooked. When he finally drove away, I was waving from the front stoop, secure in the knowledge that I had his beeper number written in ballpoint on my inner thigh. General Beauregard was under the weather, too, and for two days after Apache left he urinated everywhere.

I received calls almost every day after that from Apache: when he settled down on a vibrating bed in a Motel 6 after a long day of travel, he liked to reach out and touch me. On December 24—which he, unlike Russell, had noticed was a holiday—he sent me a box of chocolates and three bottles of Bombay Sapphire, necks wrapped in fresh mistletoe. I gave a small bowl of the gin to Beauregard, who has a fine palate for spirits. We sat together in the near-empty living room on a couple of folding chairs and savored my libation of choice while watching *A Christmas Carol* on TV. I had gussied up Beauregard with a red ribbon.

On Christmas morning I helped two fellow citizens—representing, I think, the P.B.—remove the deluxe food processor I had sold them from my kitchen. While we were packing it into bubble wrap together at the kitchen table, a news story came on the radio about G.B.'s courageous Iran-Contra pardons. I clapped my hands in childish delight when I heard, causing my fellow citizens to stare at me.

G.B. had ended his reign the way he began it back in

Panama City, with utter consistency. He had said with quiet dignity that Christmas Eve, while all his enemies were sleeping, "The prosecutions of the individuals I am pardoning represent what I believe is a profoundly troubling development in the political and legal climate of our country: the criminalization of policy differences."

This was the crowning touch to his brilliant public-service career, and when I read his statement in the paper, after my clients had left with the Cuisinart, it was as though I had found a true relic in my stocking. It harkened back to the strange bond that had existed between G.B. and me and affirmed what we had shared.

For I have had policy differences myself at times, with my fellow Americans. I am not always in complete agreement with the laws of the land, as they apply to me. In the noble pursuit of life, liberty, and prosperity there are often extenuating circumstances; thus it has always been the rule of utility, rather than the precise letter of legislation, that has guided me. Accordingly, as you may have noticed, I have frequently set my own policy. For example, in re: plastic explosives at the factory. And it was gratifying to know, beyond a shadow of a doubt, that G.B. endorsed this choice. He was waving the rippling flag of freedom to all Americans who, like me, are committed amateur policy analysts and formulators. One small step for G.B., one giant leap for your average citizen like me.

With the bold pardons he had penned his own Presidential obituary, and it was typical of his trademark sly daring and his Firm Resolve. In a democracy, we all must help ourselves; we all must take the initiative. Each single private citizen is like a flowering tree with three branches: legislative, executive, and judiciary. As long as we are patriots— and he said as much himself—we will make it to heaven eventually.

And it is only there, I came to see finally on Christmas, 1992, that I will truly come to know G.B.

Yes, a sense of loss came with this recognition; yes, something irreplaceable had been taken from me. Still, I was going to let it end cleanly—for now. I would let our ties be severed by Destiny; but only temporarily, until we both were dead.

And I would say, "G.B. is dead; long live G.B."

Because in the afterworld G.B. will always be a President. There he will stand in a stately, martial line, chin proudly raised, shoulder to shoulder with others of his stature: Genghis Khan, Julius Caesar, Richard M. Nixon. And there I will greet him exuberantly. My people the G.P. will stand behind me in all their billions, many of them wearing clothes from outlet stores along the interstate. Dead, they won't have to work for a living. And with the time that that gives them, they'll have reflected on a number of things. As a result, after a brief consultation, they will beg to tear him limb from limb.

But I will prevail; I will be the peacemaker. And finally we will all sit down together at an endless banquet table, eat milk-fed veal, and laugh out of the sides of our mouths at the petty troubles of the ones who are alive.

Epilogue

I watched the Inauguration of President 42 from my new used armchair in a trailer I had just rented outside Charlotte, NC. I had picked the armchair up at a yard sale for ten dollars, after testing the springs by bouncing on them repeatedly. It was a little frayed along the headrest, but still serviceable.

By that time I'd rejoined our nation's stalwart work-force. I had hit the road from the Capital on New Year's Day, and when I stopped for a burger along the highway, a bare six hours later, I happened to hear a guy at the counter say they were hiring at a golf-cart plant in an industrial park about twelve miles away. I had been planning on Tennessee, but let the chips fall where they may.

I still had my Town Car and my wide-screen TV. The former raised a few eyebrows when I drove it onto the gravel lot the day of my entrance interview; to this day I keep it neat as a pin and have the tires rotated regularly. I could have sold it, of course, but it had taken a big hit in depreciation that first year, and I figured I might as well keep it. Although I was suffering, admittedly, from reduced circumstances where lodgings were concerned, I would continue to travel in style. The driver's seat in a Town Car is proportioned generously.

Exhausted by the roller coaster of political life, I had been paying little mind to the preparations for the transition to our New Democrat regime. Apache would be arriving on Valentine's Day for a two-week stay, and I was looking forward to that. We were a nineties couple, with a bicoastal lifestyle.

But when B.C. said, "Let us begin with energy and hope," I sat forward and cast aside the *TV Guide* I had been highlighting. I've cut down on my hours considerably; I have my addiction under control. But I'm still allowed some TV.

His small, alert eyes, couched in the puffy folds of mature concern that signal integrity, caught me and held me. His smile, like Elvis Presley's, suggested a potent and luxurious libido; his down-home, all-American cheerfulness bolstered me. I was transfixed, even transmogrified.

"We have heard the trumpets. We have changed the guard," he said, and as a shiver of anticipation gripped me, I clutched a hand to my deep-buried heart and bowed my head reverently. Upward, onward, to all of us. Here was a true native son. Little Rock, Arkansas, is not Greenwich, CT. No, sir. It is a hell of a lot closer to me.

As the new First Family danced, and Baby Boom music blared jubilantly, I nursed my cold Red Dog with General Beauregard sleeping peacefully beside me. (Though barely out of his youth, he had already grown immensely large, and now moves ponderously when he moves at all. Chiefly he moves in the direction of his food dish.) I sang along in what approximated a waking dream state, gazing at the cherubic face of B.C., and I smiled.

The General Public would follow B.C.: he was young, ravenous in his appetites, and more boyish still than G.B. He would promise eternally, and with greater sincerity. My people are pragmatic; and like my fellow members of the G.P. I ask not what I can do for my country, but what my country can do for me.

A new era, not unlike the old, was beginning.

LYDIA MILLET grew up in Toronto. She graduated from the University of North Carolina and holds a master's degree from Duke University's School of the Environment. She is the author of *Omnivores* and has contributed to *The Baffler, The Guardian,* and *The Amicus Journal;* her work also appears in *Mirror, Mirror on the Wall,* an anthology of essays by women. She lives in Tucson, Arizona, and New York City.